"Your nose stays as it is."

"Daddy," I start one night as we two are alone in the living room and Mom is off in the kitchen. "I know Mom talked to you about my nose and the operation I'm thinking of, and I know you were against it. Have you thought about it, and — maybe — changed your mind?"

"I have thought about it, but I haven't changed my mind. The answer is still no. No operation. Your nose stays as it is. It's the classic Trevor nose. It's been passed along for generations. No one ever complained about it before."

"But it makes me unhappy."

"It shouldn't."

"You can't tell a person that something that bothers her shouldn't bother her."

"I'm telling you exactly that. This preoccupation with your nose will pass away. You'll forget about it. . . ."

The conversation ends there, and I kiss him goodnight. There is nowhere we two can go. . . .

D0829751

Other Point paperbacks
you will enjoy:

The Empty Summer
by Caryl Brooks

Dancing on Dark Water
by Alden Carter

Until Whatever
by Martha Humphreys

Life Without Friends
by Ellen Emerson White

point

RHINO

SHEILA SOLOMON KLASS

SCHOLASTIC INC.
New York Toronto London Auckland Sydney

ISBN 0-590-44251-1

12 11 10 9 8 7 6 5 4 3 2 1   6 7 8 9/9 0 1/0

Printed in the U.S.A.   01

For Josephine Charlotte Paulina Wolff
— indomitable from the word go

RHINO

ONE

When I look in the mirror on my wall, I don't expect to see Snow White, the fairest of them all. I know life is no fairy tale. But I always hope for more than I get.

What I get is an okay face and in the middle of it a clunky nose. I can't deal with myself as a girl with that kind of nose. I'm a size nine, nicely shaped, curvy. I shop in junior shops and that's the way I like to think of myself — petite (maybe even cute some days) — but ever since I was twelve years old I've been aware of my nose.

Fats Russell first brought it to my attention.

I was in sixth grade then. It was after three o'clock one school day, and a bunch of us had stopped for pizza on the way home. Fats must have been sitting at the counter. I never noticed him.

We were crowded into a booth, and I was asking

silly-question jokes. I loved to make them up. "What do baby mice rinse out with after they brush their teeth?" I waited. "Mousewash."

There were groans and laughs.

"What did Prince Hamlet say to the overweight woman?" I gave them a second. "Tubby or not tubby."

My friends cracked up, and then, suddenly, Fats was standing there looking at me mean, and saying, "What's so funny, Bump? Yeah. That's what they should've named you with that nose. Bump!"

"Get off it, Fats," my girlfriends protested. "Nobody invited you over here."

I didn't speak. I was devastated.

"So long, Bump!" he said, and I just sat there, silent. He stopped on the way out to turn around. "Bump!" he said, lifting his hand and cocking his thumb and then shooting my nose with his finger. "Bump!" Then I watched him go out the swinging door after he'd ruined my life.

My friends guessed maybe he was jealous because we were having fun, or maybe he thought we were laughing at him, and a whole lot of that kind of stuff, but it didn't help. That afternoon in the pizzeria changed my life. I went home and looked in the mirror, and Fats was right.

It's stupid that it should bother me so much. I'm not totally a coward, and I try not to be a phony. My folks just about manage for money with both of them working. Our house is comfortable, but run-down, and my mother is forever saying how proud she is

▼

we make do. That means we don't owe anyone a lot. For us, dinner out is Kentucky Fried Chicken or Pizza Hut, and I love it, all of us together, with Mom sitting instead of getting up and down a million times. I was raised to be what I am, not to pretend.

What I am is a girl who hates her nose.

"You're pretty," my boyfriend tells me lots of times. He likes me just as I am. Period. B.B. (Before Bob) I used to fantasize that that would be paradise, a steady boyfriend in high school, a good-looking guy, a senior! (Actually, we didn't meet in school; we met demonstrating how to make chestnut croquettes in YIN/YANG/YUMMY, the natural-food supermarket where we both work part-time.) Anyway, I thought when a boyfriend came along, the nose problem would vanish. But it didn't.

Bob is a photography freak. He has a Nikon for serious pictures and a Polaroid for candids, both bought with money earned working nights, Saturdays, holidays, summers. To him a camera is like an American Express Card. He can't leave home without it. Bob loves to take pictures of me, so I can't be a total turkey. Some of the photos he takes are really flattering — the unposed, happy shots. None in profile.

All this should take the curse off, but it doesn't. When something is wrong with the bod or the mind, anyone outside of you telling you nice things about yourself is about as distant as the Arctic Circle. What's going on inside your head is really all that counts. I make it through each day doing all the normal stuff: school, a few household chores, jogging, homework, watching TV. An average American teenager.

All the while, underneath, I am asking the same desperate question over and over: *God, why did you do this to me?*

Since I spend a lot of time thanking Him and talking to Him, I consider it my right to complain. I believe He hears me.

I wonder if, inside their heads, other kids are like this, too. The loud ones, the shy ones, the nasty ones — even Fats Russell — the clowns and the jocks; are they all constantly asking WHY?

Whoever said adolescents have it made?

TWO

"Acid rain is destroying the forests and foliage and killing the ducks," Ms. Campion tells us.

"No more animal quackers!" Fats calls out, and one or two of the creeps who hang out with him laugh. We are in our Living course, Edison High School's attempt to deal with the real world.

"Acidic lakes can't support much aquatic life. Fish and ducklings compete for food, and the fish are faster."

"Good-bye Donald and Daisy." Fats again. *"Au river*, Daffy."

He has to keep interrupting. He is so proud he is taking French, he has to show off.

I also am taking French. *"En avant,"* I grumble.

"Ferme-la, Bump!" he shoots back at me.

"That's quite enough, William." Ms. Campion zaps him with a look. She may be the only one left who remembers his name is not Fats. She tries to end the lesson upbeat. "We have to be active environmentalists," she urges, pacing up one aisle and down another and never standing still. I guess she figures a moving object is less likely to lull students to sleep. I don't think she's dull; I think she's terrific, but a lot of my classmates are just sitting out high school. A few are nodding out.

"We have to fight the pollution of our earth, the smog in our cities, and — cigarette smoke in our immediate environment." School bathrooms is what she means. "The spoilers must not inherit the earth or the air. Or the washrooms of Edison Regional High School." She gets a laugh from the nonsmokers, most of us; she gets smirks and an under-the-desk finger from several of the others.

I feel bad about the ducks. I think they're cute in a special way. Take swans, for example. They're beautiful and graceful, but they aren't funny the way ducks are, and they haven't a quack in them. Or a peep. Or, take ostriches. They're nice, but weird. I mean an ostrich can grow eight feet tall and weigh three hundred pounds.

How do I know all this? Grandpa taught me years ago. Every spring, on Sundays, he used to take me to the Bronx Zoo. In those days he was fascinated by animals and stars and planets and peculiar tropical fish. No more. He's in a life-and-death struggle now with smoking — he says it's the only monkey he ever had on his back — and he hates it. But I remember those happier times, when Grandpa could breathe, as he says, "like a man."

▼

"He's cute," I said once, admiring an immense strutting ostrich.

Grandpa laughed. "Annie, no one could call that fellow cute."

"What would you call him, Grandpa?"

"One of Mother Nature's tricks." He handed me a silver helium balloon. "How this balloon stays up is another trick. The old girl is full of surprises." He always talked about Mother Nature as if she were one of his buddies. "Now, let's take our breadcrumbs to the lake and feed the ducks," he suggested. Duck-feeding was my favorite part of the whole outing next to what Grandpa called Annie-feeding, from a Cracker Jack box that held a prize.

Okay. So I identify with ducks.

Ms. Campion is gathering up her books and papers. "William — " She nabs him before he can escape, and she chews him out quietly for rudeness. I strain my ears to enjoy every reprimand, every single sharp word.

I sit there wondering if I will ever be energetic and optimistic like Ms. Campion. And tough, too. She's got Fats listening to her.

She's a fresh-looking young woman, I guess about thirty or so. Her clothes are all loose and baggy. She's into denim and natural fibers. Her long brown hair hangs in a soft braid. She's not stylish, yet she has a style of her own. Everything interests her, and she's always ready to join a battle. Clean air! Clean water! Pure foods! Ban tobacco! Preserve landmark buildings! Put air bags in cars! Save the whales!

I have some good days when I'd be glad to march

▼

behind her. But then I have other days when I hate everyone and everything, when I blame Mom and Dad for my genes and I envy my sister Kate, who's beautiful, and I wish I had been born somewhere else some other time: Paris, when I could have been part of the French Revolution along with Madam Defarge (I can knit); or London, as a noblewoman at Elizabeth the First's court. So what if I could have had my head chopped off in Paris, or caught the plague in London? (Ms. Campion says they had open sewage ditches running alongside the streets. Yuck.) Even so, those were the good old days. Any days before these acid-rain days must have been better.

Fats actually reaches to carry the teacher's books and papers. It's a miracle! I sit way back and pretend to be passing out from shock as they depart.

It's the last class of the day, and I am in no hurry because Bob is coming by. Right next to me, Dee takes her glasses off and quickly snaps them into their case. Dee has worn glasses since she came into my class in first grade. She's very pretty — tall, green eyes, honey-blonde hair — and she's amazing in math, but all she has to hear is what a brain she is, and she's wasted. I understand because I've been around since they first called her "Four-eyes." Her mother, who's dying for Dee to be the great brain of the century, won't spring for contact lenses. "What do you care about glasses?" she keeps saying. "Einstein wore glasses, and it never hurt him." (What an argument to use against Fats and the other bullies.)

"Yeah, did you ever see a picture of how Einstein

looked?" is Dee's answer. "Someone should have treated him to a comb."

Her mother is not interested.

Ninety percent of the time, Dee walks around with her glasses tucked away. Blind.

"Bye. I've got to take off fast for my baby-sitting job," she tells me, and she runs. These days she's practically a one-woman day-care center. She's figured out a way to cut the Einstein connection. She's saving her own money for contacts.

"Watch the lights at the crossing," I call after her. Without her specs she's an endangered species. I'll be so glad when she gets her lenses. She turns to give me a quick grin, and she's gone.

The room is almost empty. What happens next is even more depressing than the demise of the ducks.

I stuff my books into my backpack and am just shrugging into my jacket when Vickie Upham, a ditsy new girl — who wears her mouth frosted in baby-pink and has the longest, reddest fingernails I ever saw — asks, "Hey, there, Annie. What happened to your nose?"

Among the civilized people of the world, that question does not get asked. It belongs in the same forbidden category as: Does your father beat your mother? How far do you go with boys? Do you do drugs? I mean — you don't go around asking such gross personal questions, particularly during your first weeks in a new school. You settle in first. You meet people. You make friends. And even then . . . ?

Vickie is tall and hippy with a hollow chest and

sucked-in cheeks, like some bizarre high-fashion model. Her clothes shout Designer! Import! Money! That was surely what made her so careless in her question. We have a word for that around here; we call it *chutzpah*. No surprise she's a midterm transfer to our school. They must have thrown her out somewhere else. For abusing substances and/or people.

I frown thoughtfully. "Nose?" I say gingerly, as if it is some foreign word. I look at her in astonishment and stall for time. Where is Bob? "What nose?" I am too shook up to do better than that.

An uncertain smile flickers on her glistening lips. My answer has confused her. (It's so stupid.)

"*My* nose? Whatever can you be talking about?"

Enter the hero, beautifully timed. "Yeah," he says, striding toward us, "whatever — ?" Never was a knight more welcome.

Vickie begins to shift her feet uneasily, as if her toes are pinched. Maybe the Reeboks are too small. She does have big feet. Big feet seem to go with pea brains a lot of times. Somebody ought to study the connection. When she first bad-mouthed my nose, no six-foot-tall male senior was present. No blond, muscular, slim-waisted, blue-eyed male, a canvas camera bag slung over one shoulder, was standing there looking at her speculatively. Mr. Collins, my English teacher, who has just finished *Hamlet* (and I mean finished; he did the whole play in) with our class, claims that the audience reaction changes the play; different audiences make for different performances and alter the characters and the meaning. So, here, too.

▼

Vickie does a turn at wide-eyed surprise, trying to shift from witch to ingenue. "Well" — she coos — "I only meant it's like broken." She pauses and looks at Bob and me — more at Bob — waiting for acceptance and mercy. We don't give her anything but our disgusted attention.

Speaking of ostriches. Buried up to her head already, she proceeds to dig herself in deeper. "I mean, there's this bump — "

Bob and I stand as if hypnotized.

"Your nose looks as if it was once broken," she spills it out all in a rush.

I blink the old silky eyelashes at her. My lashes are thick, curly, and brown. When I work at it, I can raise a small breeze of innocence. "My nose was never broken, Vickie."

"It's a family heirloom," Bob tells her.

She shifts her feet again, as if she feels the need to put distance between us, but we aren't quite finished. Following Bob's brilliant lead, I put a hand on her hundred-fifty-dollar Benetton suede-and-wool camel cardigan and keep her there while I explain. "It's my heritage from my paternal line."

"That means her grandfather passed it along through her father to her," Bob adds helpfully.

I reinforce him. "Yes, it's a gift from my grandfather."

"But isn't he also *your* grandfather?" she asks Bob.

"I can see why you would think that," he says, managing a deadly serious tone. "Annie's short, and I'm tall. Annie's a redhead, I'm blond. Hazel eyes," he points to me. "Blue," he points to himself.

▼

Ever see a cornered rat gnaw her baby-pink lower lip? Her thinking is that because Bob is such a gorgeous handsome hunk, surely he could not be anyone but my brother picking me up after class. *My* thinking is: May she turn green and moldy for that; may her glands swell and her chest shrivel even further; may those fancy, manicured nails break; may she get a lifetime crotch itch. Nothing big, just little petty annoyances.

She leaves us.

"Moron," Bob says. "Who is she?"

"A new student."

"She really knows how to come into a place and make friends."

He's sweet, but he can't talk away my utter misery. No matter how hard I try, no matter how many times I tell myself that the way people look is only a little part of them, not the most important part, I'm vulnerable. I crumble under attack. I stay silent now.

"Annie?"

"The world is full of Vickies, and I'm not sure I want to go through life fighting the War of the Noses." I stop abruptly. I had thought of it that way, privately, and the first time I said War of the Noses to myself I even giggled, but it was no joke. I'd never said it aloud to anyone before.

Bob grins. "You know, Annie, there's no way to stop dumb people, no way to shut them up."

"In this case, there happens to be a way. I've been thinking about it a lot."

"What do you mean?"

▼

"Plastic surgery."

"Ha. That's the rich man's way. It's incredibly expensive."

"I know. But if I put in more hours at YIN/YANG/ YUMMY — I could give up the extracurricular stuff after school — and if I am real careful with my money, I might be able to pay for it. The big question is, should I do it?"

"So that's why you've been talking about giving up the school paper. But you love working on it! You'd be willing to junk that?"

"If I have to. Bob, should I have my nose fixed? I'm asking you for the brutal truth. Would you consider it a cop-out?"

He's slow to answer. "I really don't know. I'll have to think about it, about what a major change to your face would do to you."

"Make me pretty?" My voice is shaky.

"You're pretty now. Your features are irregular, but I think you have an interesting face."

"Would you say that to Miss America or to any movie star?" I shake my head. "No girl in her right mind wants an interesting face. Not *interesting* and not *unusual*. Those are killer words."

"You're off-base, Annie."

"Maybe. But I can't help it. I'd rather be more usual. What I want most is to be pretty. I'm not asking to be beautiful, just pretty."

"Look at Ms. Campion. She's fascinating to listen to. Nobody seems to care that she's not pretty — or that she dresses in tents and wears her hair like her

▼

grandmother used to. Kids die to get into her classes, even though she makes them work. You know she's not an easy marker."

He's so crazy about her because she wants to save the world, and because she loves photography and is a film buff like he is. Sometimes I'm almost a little jealous.

"Interesting and unusual are okay for a mind, not a face. Maybe when I'm thirty I'll want to be like her, but not now."

All right, so she's a great teacher. The guidance counselors are always talking about role models, and here is Bob offering me a good one. But that is not the way I want to go.

I am glad to move the conversation to something else. "I had a stroke of genius last night. The great Ms. C wants a guest to come in and talk to us about alternative ideas in nutrition and health. Fats volunteered himself — "

Bob laughs. "The Fritos-Nachos-Oreos Killer Calorie diet?"

"Right. She turned him down. Then I thought of Mr. Buehler."

Mr. Buehler is our boss, the owner of YIN/YANG/YUMMY and one of our favorite people, if a bit weird. He's got shelves of nutrition books in his little office in the store, and he reads just about everything that is printed: newspapers, magazines, novels.

"He just might do it," Bob agrees. "It's a chance to spread the good word about brown rice."

"The important question is, do you think they will *like* one another?"

▼

"Fats and Mr. Buehler?"

That makes us both laugh.

Bob loves the idea of Ms. Campion and Mr. Buehler. "She's a fish-vegetarian. Perfect! They're made for each other. When sushi meets bean sprout — watch out!"

THREE

Bob and I go down the school stairs. Our fun put-down of Vickie Upham has delayed us. The whole building seems empty. A deserted school building is a dismal place inhabited by the smells and silent voices of thousands of adolescents *yearning to be free*. That's from the Emma Lazarus sonnet on the Statue of Liberty. She was writing about immigrants, but teenagers yearn for things more than anyone, I bet. And I'm the biggest yearner of all.

"Let me think about the plastic surgery question," Bob says. "It will take my mind off my own troubles."

"You? The man with the gorgeous nose? If I had a nose like yours, I'd feel like the Duke of Earl."

"Not today you wouldn't. I have some bad news. Raymond caught me reading during his idiot class discussion of checks and balances."

▼

"Not again."

"Again. 'Nobody reads during class discussion, Mr. Pritchitt.' He only calls me 'Mister' when he's on my case. He makes it sound like a dirty word: '*Misterrr!* How many times have I told you — in my classroom, you do as I say?'"

"Then, Bob, why are you here now? Why aren't you in Detention?"

"He didn't just assign Detention. He sent me to the dean."

I stop. Detention is sort of routine for Mr. Raymond's students. Anyone who does anything he doesn't like sits around for an hour after school doing "supervised study."

"How come?"

"He wants to see a parent tomorrow. My father won't let my mother come. *He's* the boss in our family."

I gasp. Bob and his father have a rocky relationship. If you can call mostly not talking to each other a relationship. Mr. Pritchitt will really not appreciate this summons.

"That's major. What happened?"

Bob looks bleak. "Things got a little confused in there for a while. He came up behind me and leaned over — maybe to grab the book out of my lap, I don't know — and he startled me, so I stood up suddenly to protect the book and bumped into his little chin, and he got scared. He must have thought I was going to hit him or some crazy thing. 'Another picture book, Pritchitt?' he cracked. You remember, last time he caught me with Karsh's *Portraits*."

I do remember. "What were you reading this time?"

"*Let Us Now Praise Famous Men*. It was written by some good writer named Agee with incredible pictures by Walker Evans. It's about the Great Depression."

"It sounds like a history book. It should be legal to read a history book in a history class."

"I tried that argument." Bob smiles ruefully. "I told him it's American history, it's about tenant farmers.

" 'But it's not about checks and balances, Mr. Pritchitt. You just take your little book and go visit the dean. I'll see your parent tomorrow.'

"So, I ended up sitting in the office for the period. Dean Packard was at a meeting, and he didn't get back till after three. When he came in, I told him you were waiting for me upstairs. He sent me up to get you." Bob looked embarrassed.

"You'd better hurry," I said. "What with Vickie and all, we've been taking our time."

"He said not to hurry, he'd be a few minutes before he could get to me. Annie — will you come along?"

"To the dean's office? He won't allow that."

"He suggested it. He said, 'Is the friend who's waiting a close friend?' I said, 'It's Annie Trevor. My best friend.' He said, 'Then bring her along. You need a friend — for moral support.' "

"Dean Packard must be tired of seeing you."

"He's cool."

Dean Packard is unusual in our school; he's our only black faculty member. Some joker named him "the fair dean," and we all call him that. He's actually *Dr.* Packard, but he doesn't go bananas if you forget his title. (The advisor to seniors, Dr. Zimmer, will blow away anyone who forgets *his* title.) The dean is known for listening to the student's side of the story: He's tough, but he's fair.

"Sure, I'll come," I agree, and we move a little faster. We get there, Bob knocks, and we enter.

"Hello, Annie," the dean greets me. "Sorry he kept you waiting up there. It wasn't his fault. He had to cool his heels down here while I was out." He points to a chair over on the side of the room, and I head for it.

"I need not remind you that this is a private conversation not meant for any other ears," the dean starts as he directs Bob to the seat right in front of his desk.

We nod.

"I have to send for your parent," the dean starts. "Mr. Raymond insists."

"Reading is no crime, Dr. Packard," Bob tries to defend himself.

"We've been over this ground before. This is the fourth time he's caught you. He determines the class's work, and he ordained that today would be a discussion period."

"Ordained?" The word slips out before Bob can stop himself. He is immediately embarrassed and very sorry.

The dean sits back in his chair, silent, and he studies Bob. "Why do you make it so hard for yourself? With your intelligence and your scores, you could

▼

go practically anywhere after high school. But so far only one teacher is willing to support you. Ms. Campion says you're a brilliant photographer. Potentially a prizewinner, she thinks. Why are you so prickly, so self-destructive?"

Bob feels terrible, I can see. "I don't want to talk about me," he mumbles. "I'm here to talk about Raymond's class."

"*Mr.* Raymond's class. And we *are* talking about you."

"The discussion was asinine, Dean Packard. We've had that same discussion in every American history class since sixth grade. Who wants to talk about checks and balances again?"

"Mr. Raymond, obviously. He decides, and he makes up his syllabus. Look, Bob. A parent has to be here tomorrow morning."

"My father won't let my mother come, and he won't want to take time off from work. He loses pay — "

"Tomorrow morning," the dean repeats quietly. "Mr. Raymond insists. I tried to talk him out of it, but he finds you threatening."

"I just stood up because he was reaching at me from behind."

"I understand. But you are recalcitrant. And you are also much bigger than he is."

"My father shouldn't have to come in because I was caught reading a great book."

"You know better than that. Your father has to come in because you broke Mr. Raymond's rules. You live in society, you learn to accept its regulations. The book *is* a great book, but in the classroom the teacher is the law. If Mr. Raymond says checks and balances, that's it. He wants your father in."

"He'll be sorry. My father is not a reasonable man."

"See you in the morning." Dean Packard rises and walks toward the door. We both get up and follow. "Annie," the dean stops me, "can you keep this fellow out of trouble — at least till graduation?"

"I'll try, Dean Packard. I'll do my best."

"I know you will. I'm glad you came along."

We go out and hear the door close firmly behind us.

"Me, too, Annie. I'm glad you were there."

I look at him and I marvel. "What I don't understand is how you could let me go on and on about my nose when *you* have *real* trouble."

"I don't want to talk about it anymore" — His voice is choked — "I just want to drop it now."

"All right. But you have to promise to tell me exactly what happens tomorrow."

He is silent.

"You brought me into this, Bob. Now I'm part of it."

"Okay, okay. You'll get it blow-by-blow. But let's leave it — now!"

He stops, and then in a really weird high tone, he says, "I might as well help you decide whether you should get scalpeled."

"Don't put it like that."

The weird tone is hysteria. He is trying desperately to erase the scene in the dean's office from our minds. Teasing is his way. "Carved?" he begins to joke.

"Snipped? Streamlined?" He tries to grin at me. "Renovated?"

We unlock our bikes. He kisses me swiftly. "I'll give you a call later," he says and rides off. "Abridged!" he shouts from the distance. He goes toward Edison, the grungy town the regional high school is attached to. I set out for Cloverdale, the bedroom suburb where my parents own a worn, old house.

He will tell me exactly what he thinks. Bob is absolutely reliable; once he knows his mind, he'll speak it even if it's not what I want to hear. While we're different in many ways, Bob and I, we believe in honesty and we trust each other.

Not that I don't trust my parents. I do. But they love me and want to protect me. They're light-years away from adolescence, concerned with their own problems, which seem largely to do with how to pay for everything we need to live. So, sometimes — in fact, fairly often — crises in my life do not get Number One Attention from them.

I happen to have many crises, almost daily and often more frequently. I understand I can't get *that* much attention. Still, if I had a daughter with a nose that bothered her as much as my nose bothers me, I — the mother — would do something about it. It would have top priority. I would devote myself to solving her problem. My mother seems to think it's minor. I have only hinted about it to her a few trillion times.

Here's the picture. My name is Annie Trevor, named for my mother. I am almost fifteen, five feet

▼

four, changeable hazel eyes, curly thick auburn hair, fairly passable skin except for about four days each month, nice full lips, straight white teeth — and an irregular nose. No, I never fell or got into a fight or had my nose broken. So, why isn't the bridge straight?

My profile breaks my heart. My mother and my sister Kate, who is twenty-two, have straight beautiful noses; they could be statues or heads engraved on coins. Kate has my coloring and hair and the most beautiful profile in the world.

I never know when the dreaded question will pop up. At a social gathering, after church, anywhere, it occurs to someone to ask, and even if it's asked tactfully, it hurts.

When I raise my hand in school and people are looking at me, I make sure to sit with my chin in my other hand with my fingers arranged to shelter my nose. At parties, I stand or sit — if I can — so people see me full-face. This body engineering occupies me so I can't pay much attention to what's going on. Big social gatherings aren't so much fun for me. Sometimes kids misunderstand when I shift around so much. They think I'm bored or not paying attention, when what I'm really doing is killing myself trying to find a less conspicuous angle for my schnozz.

Am I going to spend my whole life like this?

I have "the classic Trevor nose," an exact replica of Daddy's nose and Grandpa Trevor's nose. In a way that ties me to them and makes me love them very much.

But they are both tall men with big faces; they carry the nose better. We share the hazel eyes and long lashes, too, though Grandpa's lashes and hair are white now. Daddy's hair is mostly gone; the fur gene skipped a generation. So, I not only carry the Trevor men in my heart but in my mirror.

That complicates everything. Do I want to wipe out the family resemblance? Wouldn't that hurt their feelings? Here I have a father who is proud of me and who is basically very kind. We do argue over some things: like he says MTV videos are trash, and he hates the casual way I dress ("You look like you fell out of bed."), but compared to other fathers — like Bob's, who tells him regularly, "I never wanted any kids. I got caught." — my father is great.

And my grandfather is a master carpenter who can make cabinets, tables, bookcases, and even wood sculptures. He's really an artist. I'm nervous about doing something that might say, "I don't want to look like you or your family."

It's crummy and selfish to spend so much time on this. In a world filled with real tragedies — AIDS and apartheid, wars and the homeless — I know I should just take my problem and stuff it. And there *are* long periods of time when my mind does move away from the proboscis problem of Annie Trevor. I do think about other people and what they have to deal with.

I think about my grandfather, who is not well. He insists on working every day in his workshop (which is in the small house he built for himself, a few blocks from where we live), but he has emphysema and my father worries terribly about him.

▼

"Me and John Henry," Grandpa likes to say. "I'm going to die with the hammer in my hand, oh Lord."

"Put the hammer down, stop smoking, and goof off occasionally and you'll live a lot longer," my father advises, but Grandpa can't do it. "Son, you just don't understand. Trevor men don't die in rocking chairs. You'll see when it's your time to choose. You won't quit, either."

"But I don't do the same kind of work," my father argues. He's a bookkeeper in a publishing house. "I don't do heavy lifting. And I don't smoke. Your body can't take that kind of stress anymore."

"Take away a man's work and you take away his reason for life." Grandpa leaves out any discussion of smoking because he knows he's wrong. He's quit and gone back dozens of times. It's the great struggle — and defeat — of his life. He hates being hooked worse than anything, so he keeps trying to give it up. About work, he always ends up saying the same thing: "A man has to know he's done his day's share on this earth. Then he's earned his dinner and his beer."

Some conversations, like this one between Daddy and Grandpa, are like those musical compositions called fugues where the same theme comes back again and again, sometimes changed a little but always recognizable.

I know that my sister Kate would marry her boyfriend, Charlie, tomorrow if she could, but Charlie is scared to death of poverty. He's got a good job; he services the life-saving machines in Cloverdale Hospital. He insists they save up till they have the

▼

down payment on a house, first. Nobody blames Charlie. He's been poor all his life, but that down payment puts off marriage indefinitely. I hear Kate crying in our room sometimes, late at night.

I know that my mother comes home tired from her job as a school aide in the local elementary school — I remember how we used to bug the aides when I was there, throwing food, fighting — and her feet hurt and she has headaches, and there are many household things to do, so she's not really too involved when I start talking about my nose.

I know that Bob, whom I've been going with exclusively for the past year, has dreams of being a great photographer, but the chances of those dreams coming true are slim. His father is a construction worker, and he wants Bob in that line of work, too. Good money, he argues, and he can teach Bob all he needs to know. Mr. Pritchitt says over and over again, "Photographers are all queers." He hates the sight of Bob's cameras.

I know all this, and still I can't stand it when the Vickie Uphams of the world come at me with their *nosy* questions. It's as if I'm alone on a stage, and everyone is staring at my profile.

FOUR

Bob doesn't waste much time. He calls me up promptly at eight-thirty, right as Kate and I finish doing the dishes. A bit too early for privacy. Kate and Charlie are going to a movie, so I stall around in our room, chattering about schoolwork on the phone with Bob while my sister combs her hair, powders her beautiful nose, and sprays herself with Rive Gauche.

"I've got this English assignment," I tell Bob. "Mr. Collins wants evaluations of the Shakespeare unit. They can be anonymous, just tell him what we think. I think it's the pits. Maybe *Hamlet* is a good play, but you can't tell by reading it a scene at a time and then answering ten questions. How come there are always exactly ten questions about each scene? At least he could have showed us a movie at the end of the unit, like some of the other teachers do."

▼

"Didn't he give you the speech about movies debasing drama?"

"Twenty times."

"He doesn't believe that a movie can help you understand a play, or that movies are an art form, too."

"It's too bad," I agree. "Because most of the kids will never actually see a Shakespeare play. But they might see a movie or a video."

"He wanted to teach in a college. Thirty years here at Edison, and he doesn't know who he's teaching. He's out of touch," Bob said bitterly. He had suffered through Mr. Collins's course a year ago.

"Why does he ask for honest evaluations?"

"I told you. He's out of touch. He hopes you'll love the Bard as much as he does."

"Well, I hate to be dishonest — "

"So, be honest. Write the truth."

"He's retiring in June. He's old. Why hurt his feelings?"

"Then you'll be dishonest."

"It's not that simple, Bob."

At last, Kate goes out slamming the door, her way of announcing that the coast is clear for me to talk. I do the same for her when she and Charlie want to chirp away on the phone. You should hear them talking lovey-dovey, and they've been going together for centuries.

"All clear," I say. "Wipe out Collins. Wipe out *Hamlet*. What did your father say?"

"He isn't home yet. He must've stopped for drinks along the way. Bad news."

"I'm sorry, Bob."

▼

28

"About your schnozz. Don't do it."

"But, why — if it makes me prettier?"

"I just have this feeling," he says, "that it's — phony. A cop-out."

"I know I asked your opinion, so I shouldn't argue with it. But, Bob, shouldn't a person be happy with the way she looks? Dee hates her glasses, so she's getting contacts. That's the way everyone operates when it comes to hair, makeup, clothes. Men decide if they're going to shave or have mustaches or beards. What's so sacred about a nose?"

"It's not sacred. It's just basic, what you start out with. It's you. Mustaches and beards and those kinds of things come and go. A nose is forever. Remember, if you do it, you're stuck with it, with whatever blob they give you."

"It's true that it's permanent. And it does cost a lot. Oh, I don't know why I asked you."

"You wanted an honest opinion."

"Not really. I wanted your support when the yelling starts around here."

"Who's going to yell?"

"Only everyone. My parents will say I'm nuts. My grandfather will be convinced I'm ashamed of my heritage. Charlie will think it's a big waste of money. Kate? Well, maybe Kate won't yell. She'll just keep telling me how pretty I am now, and I just can't stand hearing that."

I rest my case. The judge, at the other end of the phone line, tries to sort it out. Finally, he delivers his verdict. "Listen, Annie. I gave you my opinion, but you don't have to agree with me or listen to your

▼

folks, either. It's your nose. By the time you have the money saved for this operation, you'll be old enough to vote. A citizen."

"Oh, no. That's three years from now. I have to get it done before then. It's on my mind — "

A door in his house slams loudly. "I have to get off now," he says. "Listen, kid, you're making a mountain out of a molehill."

"You've got it wrong. I want to make a molehill out of a mountain."

He groans.

"Good luck!" I whisper, and we hang up.

I have no plan to start my propaganda campaign immediately. But I am standing in the bathroom, looking at myself in the medicine chest mirror, wishing my usual wish, when my mother knocks on the door. "May I put some dirty laundry in the hamper?" she asks.

"Of course. Come in, it's not locked. I'm just looking at my nose."

In she comes with an armload of stuff. "I'll get the rest," I tell her, and I run upstairs for the pile of bed-linens and towels. She tries to take care of the dunderhead housework — that doesn't require a brain — at night when she's tired. My mother is a peach. She is medium height and plump; her brown eyes shine, and she smiles a lot so two dimples flicker constantly in her cheeks. I love her dearly.

"You shouldn't spend so much time staring into the mirror," she chides me.

"I was wishing my nose away."

▼

"That silliness again. How many times do I have to tell you, it's a fine, strong nose? It's your own, personal, designer nose."

Designer? She's teasing me. I have to laugh.

I help her stuff the laundry into the wicker hamper. Then she turns and gives me a quick hug.

"No one else would have it," I say.

"No one else does. No use being grumpy about it, Annie. It's what God gave you."

"I'm thinking of having God's design improved a little," I blurt out.

Mom looks at me in astonishment. It just has never occurred to her that anyone in her family would come up with such an idea. I can see that her surprise is genuine. Exotic people live in other ways. Not us. Famous entertainers alter their features casually. Michael Jackson. Cher. Elizabeth Taylor. Joan Rivers. Not us. People get divorced and then remarry immediately. People like Johnny Carson. Not us. She is comfortable in our world, not theirs.

"You're kidding," she says.

I shake my head. "I hate my nose. Why should I have to live with it? It's ugly."

"It's not ugly, darling. It's part of you." Mom strokes my hair. "You're my beautiful girl. No part of you could be ugly."

"Oh, no?" I tell her about Vickie Upham with her baby-pink mouth and her claws.

"The world is full of fools and busybodies," Mom says. "Are you going to let that stupid girl dictate to you?"

"But she's right. It's a broken nose." I want so

▼

desperately to get through to Mom, but she doesn't *hear* me. I begin to cry. "I want — a straight, beautiful nose — like normal people — have."

"There, there," she tries to calm me. She is very distressed. "Let me think about it. It's not possible right now, anyway. We simply don't have the money."

"I wouldn't ask you and Dad to pay for it. I'd use my own savings and earn the rest."

"I thought those savings were for college, Annie. You're always saying you're going to be the first Trevor with a college degree."

"This is important to me *now*, Mom. I'd start saving again right after — and I'd work hard and make the money for college. I would. It'd be worth it!"

She smiles tiredly. "We'll think about it, dear."

She means it. But she also operates on the delay theory: If you put things off long enough, they may go away, heal themselves, or whatever. She may think about it for the next ten years. It's the way grown-ups are; they have no sense of emergency.

At least she took it seriously and she's willing to consider it. I am immensely grateful for that.

I write the evaluation for Mr. Collins. I am kind and, therefore, dishonest. A hypocrite, Bob will think, when I tell him. But Mr. Collins is not a bad man; he's just dull. Bob can't forgive that in a teacher. He thinks crummy teaching is a criminal offense. That's what gets him into constant trouble in school. The teachers find him arrogant, when all he is is smart and unwilling to pretend that he's not.

▼

His SAT scores hug the eight-hundreds. You would think the faculty of Edison Regional High School would be crazy about that, but they're not. They want a little student humility, a little gratitude, which Bob won't give. He learns on his own and barely pays lip service to rote lessons. So, they don't like him. A little dishonesty would carry him a long way, but not in the direction he wants to go.

To be fair to myself, I did like *Hamlet*. The poetry was beautiful. In my essay's last paragraph, I suggest seeing the film of the play as a culminating activity. *Seeing the play on film won't spoil it for us*, I write. *It will give us an impression, a basis for comparison.* Then I do a brave thing: I sign my name. Mr. Collins said our comments could be anonymous, but I don't want to hide that way.

Bob, Mr. Collins, and Prince Hamlet are very much on my mind as I wash, brush my teeth, press my nose (I mold it with my fingers every night, trying to reshape it), and slip into my sleepshirt.

I wonder what is going on in the Pritchitt house. Depending on how many drinks Bob's father had on his way home from work, he could be anything from mildly irritated to raving furious. He's been after Bob for a while to quit school. He's afraid too much reading makes a man womanly. "There's no point in all that readin' and yakkin'," he tells Bob. "I can see it for the girls. They've got nothin' else to do. But you're better off workin'." He's trying to get Bob into construction work.

They've always had trouble with one another, and Bob says that's nothing compared to the way his grandfather treated his father. "In your family, they pass along a bumpy nose, but my folks have kids and then they make them pay forever for being born," he told me once.

His father will certainly make him pay for Dean Packard's summons. If ever there was anyone in a trap, it's Bob. What he really needs is an apprenticeship to a photographer. At the very least, he needs to finish out this year, to graduate. Then he can work and maybe study part-time. He wants so much to learn how to make films.

I fall asleep with Bob and Mr. Collins on my mind, an anxious jumble of thoughts. You'd think my dreams would be focused on one of them. No. Give my subconscious mind one second and it returns — it *runs* back — to the single most important problem of my life.

My nose.

FIVE

I dream I am leaving on a jet plane, sent by the school newspaper to interview Barbra Streisand.

Whfft! Here I am in her immense dressing room crowded with crystal vases full of long-stemmed red roses and boxes of creamy rich Godiva chocolates. I shake off my jet lag instantly at the sight of the huge, stunning, signed photographs of her leading men: Robert Redford, Omar Sharif, Nick Nolte, and Ryan O'Neal look down sexily from the walls. Nolte winks at me! I wink back.

On the dressing table is an unmistakable picture in a gold frame: her son Jason. I wink at him, too.

In she floats in a gorgeous, strapless, black-sequined gown, glittering emeralds in her ears and around her neck. A spectacular-looking woman. Apparently, she can read minds.

"You're thinking that I'm pretty, but I'd be much

prettier with a small nose," she says.

"How — did you know?"

"Let's say I see it in your eyes. And I have been interviewed by high school reporters before."

"Excuse me," I say, "but — "

"It's all right. I can see that you have an irregular nose, too. Does it bother you?" She squirts me with perfume. "Obsession," she says.

"I'm going to have it fixed."

Smiling, she offers me a chocolate. I take a wonderful pecan caramel. "Take two or three more," she urges. "They're tiny."

She is so gracious. I do as she suggests. These chocolates taste like Nestlés increased to the hundredth power. Paradise! Cherry cordial, nougat, almond crunch; I nibble away.

"So you're going to take the big step," she resumes our conversation. "It's a very individual decision. I could have had my nose altered long ago, but it doesn't bother me."

"I wish I could say that. My nose bothers me terribly."

Barbra smiles. She has a radiant smile. "I just decided when I was very young that I'd go after what I wanted. If Pinocchio could do it, I could do it!" This makes us both giggle. "I'd work hard and use all my talents to make it. Nothing would stop me." She shrugs. "And that's pretty much what I did. But I was lucky. Early in my career I met a man — Marty Erlichman — who offered to be my manager. He said it wasn't necessary to change anything: not

my nose, not my voice, nothing. So I stayed me."
She pirouettes around madly.

"Didn't you ever weaken — not once?"

"Well," Barbra says, "and this is not for the school
newspaper. Actually, I did once. I let them airbrush
the nose on the cover of my second album. I've been
sorry ever since. But that was the only time," she
says fiercely. "Remember, beauty is in the eyes of
the beholder. Years ago, when I was just starting
out, Hedy Lamarr sent me a note backstage. You
know what she wrote? 'Dear Barbra, You make Elizabeth Taylor look like an old bag. Love, Hedy.' That
message has waved in my memory like a banner ever
since."

"You remind me of my grandfather," I say.

"Why, does he have a big nose?"

"As a matter of fact, he does, but that wasn't what
I meant. I was talking about his character. He's a
strong person."

"It's got nothing to do with strength. Don't put
yourself down. It's very personal. If your nose bothers you so much, you need to change it. That's all."
She begins to hum "Don't Rain on My Parade," and
I listen, amazed at the beauty and power of her voice.
She really belts the song out now, and I am her only
audience. It's like a command performance.

So far it's been practically all an interview of *me*.
I get ready to ask her some vital questions as soon
as her singing is finished.

What's it like to kiss Nick Nolte?

Who is sexier, Robert Redford or Ryan O'Neal?

▼

Which one is your favorite leading man?

What is your favorite song?

Do you know the silly-question joke about you? *What is the name of the movie starring Barbra Streisand as a young Chinese student who wants more than anything else to study Talmud?* (The answer is Ori-Yentl.)

I am smiling in my dream when my sister Kate comes tiptoeing into our room and I wake up. "Hi," I say groggily. "Barbra Streisand just told me to get my nose bobbed. I'm going to do it."

"You're in another world, Annie. Go back to sleep," Kate whispers.

"She really did," I insist. "She's terrific." I duck my head down under the covers and try to pick up the wonderful dream again, so I can get to ask my questions, but it is gone.

In the morning as we are dressing, Kate looks at me curiously. "You said the oddest thing to me last night in your sleep. You said Barbra Streisand had just advised you to get your nose bobbed."

"She did. I met her in a dream, and that is exactly what she advised."

Kate is brushing her hair. She and I have this thick tangly hair that has to be tamed each morning. "Doesn't make any sense to me," she says, "since *she* never touched her own nose. And hers is a lot worse than yours."

One thing about my sister Kate, she is loyal. All my life she has been on my side and she's stood up for me. In the War of the Noses, Barbra and I are

▼

both losers. But it's nice to have Kate as an ally.

"Barbra said she always knew she could make it on talent and hard work, so her nose never really troubled her."

"Doesn't your dream-Barbra think *you* can make it on talent and hard work?"

"She says it's not what anyone else thinks that matters. It's an individual thing. It's what *I* think. And *I* think I want to be rid of this nose."

Kate comes up behind me and puts her arms around me and gives me a squeeze. "Poor baby, does it bother you that much?"

"Yes. That much."

"The thing is, it's chancy. And expensive — thousands of dollars. I'd say Charlie and I would help you out, but at the rate we're saving now" — she sighs — "if I offered any of it to you, the wedding would be postponed till the twenty-first century."

"Kate, I wouldn't touch your money. If I decide to do it, I'll pay for it. I can work after school. I already have nine hundred dollars saved from birthday presents and baby-sitting and stuff. I'm just so unsure about the operation. I go to sleep with one nose; I wake up with another. And that's the one I have forever."

"Let me talk to Charlie about it," she suggests as she buttons her white shirtwaist and straightens her skirt. "Because he works in the hospital, he sees a lot of nose jobs."

"I hate that phrase."

"That's what they're called, honey. You'd better get used to the words and the idea if you're going to do it. You can't pretend nothing's happening."

I agree. The truth — that I will have to live with the Vickie Uphams and the Fats Russells of the world and their comments no matter what — is not anything I like to dwell on. I am concentrating on the best possible ending: Happily ever after!

The questions won't ever stop. They'll just be different questions.

"Let me find out what Charlie thinks."

"Good idea, Kate. Ask him if the patients come out with really classy noses. Ask him if it hurts a lot. Ask him if he knows a super plastic surgeon, one of the best."

"One of the best is going to cost, baby."

I rub the offensive feature. "I can't take a chance on bargains. If I really have it done, it must be done by a master, an artist."

Kate laughs. "Gotta run." She's a secretary in a law firm, and her boss, who is otherwise normal and nice, is never a minute late. She blows me a kiss. "I'll tell Charlie we want the Michelangelo of noses!"

SIX

I get to school early, walking with Dee. I am her Seeing-Eye Guide, filling her in on who's walking with whom across the street and pacing her as we brave the morning traffic. She has been going on about tinted contacts that will change the color of her eyes, which are a lovely sea-green, so I think she is crazy to do it. We are arguing over whether blue or green eyes are sexier — a really heavy question — when we see Bob and his father waiting in the main corridor outside the administrative office.

Mr. Pritchitt is in his denim work-clothes and electric-blue hard hat. He's a big man with a beer belly and a flushed face, thinning blond hair, and pale blue eyes. He's always redfaced, as if he's been running. Always. Bob says it's from drink. Bob is also tall and pale-eyed, but he's muscular and his face is bony. His father, oddly, has the baby fat. The

▼

41

differences between them are as striking as are the similarities.

Bob hates it that he looks like his father, but, in a way, it saves his life. Mr. Pritchitt, who doesn't trust anyone — ANYONE — knows by looking at Bob that he's his son.

Before coming to school, Mr. Pritchitt must have tanked up, because he's acting oddly, pacing and muttering to himself while Bob sits hunched over on the dean's bench. Everyone coming into the building through the main entrance sees them. Everyone stares. Everyone knows.

Picture it. Bob, the senior who's so private, he got into trouble for refusing to write an autobiographical essay in English class (they're read aloud). Sitting there in agony.

And that is only the beginning of the morning. . . . It zooms rapidly downhill. . . .

After school Bob's waiting, and, as I start for home, he walks his bike beside me so we can talk. Once we are away from the schoolyard, I say, "Okay. Tell me."

"You sure you want to know?" he says bleakly. "You'll be sorry you asked."

"I want to know, Bob. I'm sure."

"I'll give it to you blow-by-blow." He gulps a throat full of air and begins. His story comes pouring out in long heavy torrents broken by abrupt silences when he is too shaken to go on. It is so real and so painful, I tremble as he talks. I feel as if I am there.

Once the dean's office door was closed, Mr. Pritchitt began to make trouble. He couldn't deal with the idea that the man in charge, a school official, was black.

But, of course, he couldn't *tell* the dean he was the wrong color. So apparently he came on hard. "I didn' come to talk to you," he explained. "I wanna see the teacher who's got the beef. He's the one I'm here to see. Not you. I got nothin' personal against you."

The dean was calm. "I understand, Mr. Pritchitt, but I'm the one who sent you the note."

Mr. Pritchitt seemed dazed by that. "You're *over* the teacher?"

"I'm the dean."

"Doesn' matter. Where's the guy with the beef?"

"I usually handle student matters," the dean said.

Mr. Pritchitt wasn't impressed. "No way," he said. "I wanna see God A'Mighty himself — the teacher. I'm a parent. I got rights." He planted his two feet far apart and made it plain he wasn't going anywhere.

Dean Packard saw he'd come up against an immovable object. "I'll see if Mr. Raymond can leave his class for a few minutes," he said. "Please sit down."

Mr. Pritchitt didn't budge. He just stood there with his hat on, mad.

Surprise, surprise! It turned out that Mr. Raymond was willing to come. Eager to come. Bob's theory is that he was teaching you-know-what to another suffering class and was glad to escape. He was aggrieved. Bob had violated his jurisdiction — his favorite word for dictatorship in the classroom. In he hurried behind the dean, looking pretty pathetic:

▼

round face, bald head, round little belly under a vest, round, wire-rimmed eyeglasses, a munchkin next to oversized Mr. Pritchitt.

Then the interview really picked up steam.

"You got nothin' better to do than send for parents?" Mr. Pritchitt put it straight to the teacher. "Whasamatta with you? Whadya want out of us — blood? My kid didn' beat up on no one. His mother says he gets good grades. She woulda come herself, but I wouldn' let her. She don' know her rights. I know my rights. Whydja have to haul me in here?"

Mr. Raymond was not fazed. "Your son is undisciplined. He does as he pleases. He does not respect the rules." He glanced over at the dean for support, but the dean was staying out of it. He gave Mr. Raymond a look that said: Your game. You deal with it.

Mr. Raymond went on. "I have caught Robert repeatedly doing all sorts of things — other than my assignments — in my classroom."

Mr. Pritchitt looked him dead in the eye. "Maybe your class is borin'."

Well, when Bob is at this point in his story, I begin to shake with the giggles and then I explode. Bob is laughing, too, now, right along with me. His father was too much.

"Let's sit," I suggest, "so I can really really listen."

He agrees.

We were across the street from JFK Memorial Square, a tiny local park where there are always some secluded, empty benches because people mostly prefer sitting on their own porches or in their own gardens. Early mornings and evenings bring out

▼

the dog walkers. Now we have the place to ourselves. He lays the bike down, we sit on a bench, and the story is continued.

Mr. Raymond pretended the "borin'" remark hadn't been made. But Bob nearly cracked up. He managed to keep control of himself by looking up at the ceiling lights. It was the closest he ever came to wanting to shake his father's hand, he said.

"This time Robert had material on his lap that he was brazenly reading right through a class discussion," Mr. Raymond said indignantly.

Mr. Pritchitt put on a good show. "No!" he said loudly, rapping his knuckles against his metal hat and pretending to be horrified. "What was it — porn? *Penthouse? Hustler?* Somethin' hot?"

Mr. Raymond screwed up his nose, offended, but he didn't back off. "It was a book, a kind of documentary — with photographs. The contents are not the point. The point is that he was not doing *my* work. He was not involved with the required assignment."

Mr. Pritchitt was not too steady. He lurched a step forward at this point, and Mr. Raymond backstepped two or three steps, hastily. It was like some crazy ballet.

Mr. Pritchitt smelled the teacher's fear. Bob says that's when his father always moves in for the kill — when he's got someone scared.

"Don' be afraid of me, Teach," he mumbled. "I'm with you. I say all the time don' waste your time with books and pictures. They won' make you a red cent. I'm on your side, Teach. But I thought in school you

▼

push kids to read. In my days, that was all the teachers yammered about — read, read, read. I'm no reader myself. I use my time for more important things. That's why I cut out of school soon's I could. *Life* teaches you, not readin'. I *can'* believe your beef is he *reads* too much."

Mr. Raymond adjusted his tie. "It is not the reading itself that is objectionable, Mr. Pritchitt. It is that he reads what *he* wants to read instead of what is required of him. He's a rule-breaker, a loner."

At this point, I move closer on the bench to Bob, and I take his hand. He is deeply immersed in his memory of the scene. He is reliving it. My movement doesn't break into his story. He is busy mimicking the precise speech of his nutty history teacher.

"When I attempted to take the illicit book from him, he became aggressive."

Mr. Pritchitt digested all those words slowly, and then he broke into a grin. "You mean he took a poke atchya?"

"Not exactly. He was menacing."

"It woulda surprised me, Teach."

At every repeat of that *Teach*, a muscle in Mr. Raymond's cheek twitched. Then things really got cute. Mr. Pritchitt began to shadowbox, throwing punches in the air. "I tried to show him how to use his fists, but he's no fighter. He's no danger to a cockaroach. He sure wouldn' pick on no old teacher half of his size."

Mr. Raymond had had enough. "I've left my homeroom class uncovered. I've made my position clear, so if I may be excused —"

▼

"You wanna leave the room, Teach?" Mr. Pritchitt was enjoying himself.

"I'll take over," Dean Packard said, and Mr. Raymond literally ran.

"That man don' know there's a real world out there," Mr. Pritchitt crowed. "Look, er — er — "

"Dean Packard. Dr. Packard — "

"Yeah, doc — er — well, I been sayin' for a'least a year now that the boy's wastin' his time here. He's big. He can do a man's work. I could care less about his messin' around here. You don' wan' him in your school no more? Throw him out." He became enthusiastic. "I was workin' at his age, and it din' do me no harm. I'm not comin' back here no more, so don' send for me. If I had my way, he wouldn' come back, either. What's it good for, anyway? In the end, it's the buck that counts. And construction workers make good bucks."

He turned to Bob. "You got any sense in your head, you'll just walk out that door with me and never come back. You don' have to listen to this education garbage. These people don' know *what* they want. You read in a class, and they throw the book at you." That struck him as hilarious. Clamping his hat down on his head, he started to leave, laughing.

"Mr. Pritchitt" — Dean Packard's tone was sharp — "let me keep you one minute more. You have a very smart son. He has top test scores. He can be anything he wants to be. One of our teachers believes he'd make a great photographer. But it's hard to do alone. He needs family support."

Mr. Pritchitt didn't want to hear that. He turned,

and he pointed a finger at the dean. "You listen to me. No kid of mine is goin' to end up snappin' pretty pictures for a livin'. If he's so smart, he'll make a great construction worker. We're not dummies, you know. Smart pays off in my line, too." He headed out, making sure to slam the door.

Suddenly, Bob stops talking. He just sits there beside me, looking drained. Exhausted.

"You can tell me the rest later," I say. "You look beat."

"Oh, no. Here comes the best part," he insists. "I can't stop now." And so he continues.

After his father left, he remained where he was, humiliated. The dean didn't look at him for a while. He fussed with papers on his desk. He was giving Bob a chance to get a grip on himself after that scene which came straight out of hell.

Then the dean came up with a proposition. "If I get Mr. Raymond to agree to independent study for you, are you willing to do the readings in the school library and then take the exams? We'll find a proctor. You could even do them in this office."

In one moment, Bob said, he bungee'd up to heaven from hell. First, he sat there mute, finding the offer hard to take in. Then he told the dean, "If you arrange that, I will only be grateful to you for the rest of my life."

"It's no big deal," Dean Packard said.

"You don't know — "

The dean signalled *enough* with his hand. "Here's your book back, along with some unasked-for advice. See if you can sit on your pride and impatience till June. Just cool it, and don't screw up your possibilities."

"You still think I have possibilities? You just met my father."

"I have a father, too." The dean smiled at him. "My father is a minister."

"Ordained," Bob said uncomfortably, remembering their earlier conversation.

"Right. He's an elderly, cautious, black man who does not believe I have any future in a white suburban school. He thinks I belong in the pulpit, and he waits fearfully for the day Edison will dump me. 'First minute they don't need a token African-American, out you go,' he warns me. 'Last hired, first fired.'"

"Are you afraid that might happen?" Bob asked.

The dean shook his head. "I have faith in myself and in the system, ultimately. If I'm a token, I'm a good one. But we need to talk about you, not me. We have to convert you to a believer in your own possibilities. As long as you're alive, they are there. You've got to hang onto that idea, no matter what."

Bob was listening very carefully because his life depended on it. He took in every word. "You're no token, Dean Packard," he said. "Your father shouldn't worry. You may not be in the pulpit, but you're saving us out here. Tell him a white boy said they ought to clone you."

The dean laughed and dismissed him.

"He sent me away with more hope than I've ever felt, Annie," Bob finishes.

I lean over and hug him. I want to crush him

in that hug — that's what happens in paperback ro-
mances. Only men usually do the crushing. I'm for
equal rights, but he's twice my size.

So I do the best I can.

Which is pretty good.

That old saying should be turned around: WHERE
THERE'S HOPE, THERE'S LIFE!

SEVEN

A conversation I am not supposed to hear picks me up and then knocks me flat. I overhear it because I can't find my keys when I get home from school, so I go round the back and settle on the porch and start my French homework.

Ten minutes of deep combat with *verbes français transitifs* makes me seriously consider joining the Esperanto movement. Monsieur Simon, my French teacher — he insists on being called *Monsieur* — today spent the lesson talking about this Polish eye doctor, L.L. Zamenhof, who, in 1887 published his invented language, Esperanto. Entirely phonetic. Verbs don't change with person or number. Only SIXTEEN rules of grammar, and anyone can say anything to anyone else. Anywhere in the world. The Chinese can talk to the Eskimos! I can talk to an African or a Balinese or an Afghan! And we can all

▼

keep our own languages because Zamenhof's dream was that it should be a universal *second* language.

Monsieur Simon's tiny lapel pin, a green star on a white background, means that he is an Esperantist. He says there are more than eight million speakers in the world. And *I* have never heard of it before. We had fun giving words to him for instant translation. Love — *amo.* Boy — *knabo.* God — *Di.* A friend — *amiko.*

Sounds in the kitchen mean that Mom is home, but it's so pleasant outside, I decide to stay and finish up. Mom begins to fix dinner, Sicilian tomato sauce to go on spaghetti, I conclude from the smells making their way outside: garlic, onions, anchovies, sweet peppers with basil, eggplant, and plum tomatoes. (My nose does that part of its job remarkably well.) One of my favorite dinners is coming up. I love spaghetti and sauce, and garlicky crusty bread, and salad. Inhaling as I study makes memorizing the verbs easier. Then the kitchen conversation starts.

Dad's regular routine. "Hi, dear." Pause for a kiss. "What's new?"

"Not much. Except — "

"Except what?"

"George, what would you say if I told you that Annie needed an operation?"

"My God!" There is terror in Daddy's voice. "What's wrong?"

"Nothing. Calm down, George. I said that very badly. Annie's not sick. It's something else. Here, please taste the sauce and see if there's enough salt."

▼

52

"You are the most unbelievable woman — first you — how can I pay attention to salt — ?" Daddy sputters like a broken faucet.

"Concentrate. Hold the spoon over the sink so it won't drip, and blow on the sauce."

There is silence. I lick my lips. I adore Sicilian sauce.

"It's very good, but it could use a bit of salt. This is always your best sauce."

"Thank you."

"All right. Now what's this about Annie?"

"She's really unhappy about her nose."

There's a long silence, time for a double and perhaps even a triple take.

"Her *what*?" Daddy is astonished. Apparently, he has never noticed the problem. Maybe to parents, their children are exquisitely beautiful. Even the ugly ones.

"Her nose," Mom says. "She feels very self-conscious and embarrassed by it."

"I never heard such idiocy. She's got the Trevor nose, a fine, strong nose just like my father's and my own."

"You were never crazy about your nose, and neither was your father about his. Years ago, things were different. Plastic surgery wasn't common. And the Trevors didn't have a lot of money. But there are more possibilities now, and Annie is young enough to try them."

Mom is a dear. I haven't really convinced *her*, and here she is already doing her best to convince Dad.

That's the way she is, a softy who cares about other people's dreams. Especially her family's.

"I love my daughter just as she is, a normal, healthy, teenager. I certainly will not let her undergo any unnecessary operations."

"We're only talking about one."

"It's a crazy idea, Ann. The Trevors don't have a lot of money now, either, do they? You are talking about *thousands* of dollars." He paused. "Besides, it's just not our style."

"She has her savings, and she wants to work and earn the rest. She isn't asking us for money — only for permission."

"We aren't that kind of people, Ann. Are we?"

Mom answers slowly, thoughtfully. "Maybe there is no such thing as *that kind of people*. Maybe any person who is really unhappy about the way they look should have a chance to change."

"I love Annie's face the way it is. Nobody is going to lay a hand on her nose."

"Even if it makes her unhappy for the rest of her life?"

"It shouldn't make her unhappy."

A long silence follows, interrupted only by the clatter of a pot cover set down hard on the stove.

"Think about it," Mom urges. "It's not like you to want your children to suffer."

"Suffer!" Daddy is exasperated. "You make a big deal out of everything. So her nose isn't perfectly straight. Your teeth aren't perfectly straight. I wear glasses, and I've lost most of my hair. We manage."

▼

"She can *manage*. But what if she didn't have to manage? What if an operation could remove this problem from her life?"

"You are such a cream puff," he accuses, "that if either one of the girls came to you and asked you for anything — *anything* — you could never say no."

"Not to anything reasonable."

"You have a very elastic definition of reasonable," Daddy complains. "Whatever weird idea a child dreams up, once it's asked it becomes reasonable. I'm waiting for the day Annie wants to go alone to the moon. You'll be telling me that's reasonable."

"Women do go," Mom says. "They need training, but it's not unreasonable these days."

"I take back what I said. I had the wrong pastry. You're no cream puff." Daddy's voice has admiration in it. "Underneath, you're a tough cookie."

"Please, George" — I can tell Mom is smiling — "taste the sauce again to see if anything is missing." Silence till his mouth is full, then she pleads, "Don't close your mind." And before he can protest, "How's the flavor?"

"Perfect. Let me go wash up."

"Will you think about it?"

He makes a grumpy sound. It has some *no* in it, and maybe some *yes*. "Wait till my father gets wind of this cockamamie idea."

I can hear him leaving the kitchen, his heels heavy on the wooden floor of the hall and on the stairs. He is upset.

Jamming my books in my bookbag, I tiptoe off the

back porch and go all around the yard to arrive at the front door as if I am just coming home. "Hi, Mom." I kiss her cheek. I sniff. "Sicilian sauce! They ought to make you an honorary Sicilian."

Mom blushes with pleasure. "Want a spoonful?"

"How can you tell anything with one spoonful? You think the great chefs tell by one spoonful? I'll get a small dish."

There's no seasoning problem, of course. It's a glorious sauce. She always makes more than one dinner's worth. It gets used in omelets later on, and on English-muffin pizzas.

"I accidentally heard you and Dad talking," I confess. "I forgot my keys, so I was waiting on the back porch. Thanks for trying."

"You understand how he feels?"

"Yes. It's hopeless."

"Well — let's give it a little time. How's the sauce?"

I need several more spoonfuls to really tell. After some serious tasting, I make my decision. *"Plej fenomenega!"*

"French?" Mom is uncertain.

"No. Esperanto. An invented language that Monsieur Simon told us about today, a very easy one that everyone in the world could learn to speak. It could be a universal second language."

"What a good idea! What was that you said about my sauce?"

"Plej fenomenega. Most intensely phenomenal. Awesome."

"I like that," Mom says. "One way the whole world can say awesome."

▼

"They'd say it for this sauce."

"Oh, go ahead and take some more since you're speaking for so many others."

I head back to the magic pot. *"Mi dankas vin."* I'm about to translate.

"What an easy language," Mom says. "You're welcome."

EIGHT

I have to go and talk to Grandpa. It's not going to be easy. He has limited patience these days and only for selected topics:

- Slipshod ways things are manufactured in the United States today;

Plastic and the newest craziest way it's being used (Grandpa despises plastic);

Steinbrenner and his stranglehold on the team that could be the greatest ever;

Politicians and how power corrupts them all;

How young people today are absolute disasters because they grew up "having it too good";

Working with one's hands and how much pleasure it is.

Any one of these topics could keep him going on for hours.

I understand Grandpa, and I love him from my

▼

earliest memories of those zoo Sundays with him, and of him explaining baseball to me and teaching me how to play checkers. Grandpa was my very close friend during the first years of my life. Grandma had just died, he had lots of time, and he was lonely. We hung out together.

I press on the doorbell. It takes a while, but Grandpa eventually appears at the door. He's a tall, thin, white-haired man who still stands absolutely erect. Dressed in his work-clothes, gray cotton pants and matching shirt, he is smoking his pipe. I am sorry to see it, but I'd never say anything. Enough people remind him all the time. And he doesn't really need any reminders. He knows he's got the cough and all the other miseries that go with emphysema.

"Annie, what a nice surprise!"

"Hi, Grandpa. What did I interrupt? You working on something?"

"A bookcase with oversized shelves. For an art-book collector. Teak. Come see some really special wood."

I follow him down the three steps into the finished basement that is his workshop. It's a brightly lit room with a tiny kitchen and dinette at one end, along with a bathroom, and even a closet with a Murphy bed. The smell of the place is wood, turpentine, and varnish, a heavenly fresh combination. He's so comfortable down here, he hardly ever uses the rest of the house except to sleep, and often he even beds down next to his work. If he wakes during the night, he likes to see his latest project.

Along one wall runs a worktable with shelves over

▼

it, neatly filled with dozens of tools and jars of nails and boxes of brass handles and such. Grandpa is a careful, precise craftsman. "I'm a detail man," he says. "Fine carpentry is in the beauty of the wood and the attention to details."

I don't plan to be a carpenter, but if I ever practice any craft, Grandpa has drummed the rules of good workmanship into me: honesty, good materials, patience, taking great care, and pride in the work.

When I was small, this basement was my favorite playroom; odd bits of wood and brass handles, sandpaper and wire could all be turned into boats, castles, bird-feeders, and strange animals.

He sits down on the bench, leaving the bentwood rocker for me. Off to one side stands a tall, dark, glistening new bookcase.

"It's a beauty," I say, admiring its high, deep shelves. "What a terrific music cabinet it would make for records and cassettes and maybe, one day, CD's."

Grandpa laughs with pleasure. "You're not hinting, are you? Well, maybe for your fifteenth birthday."

"That would be the most incredible present, Grandpa . . ."

"We'll see, God willing."

We sit quietly for a while. Grandpa and I don't have to make conversation to enjoy each other's company. I feel that way with Bob, too; just sharing his company is comfortable and fun.

Finally, Grandpa focuses on me again. "Did something special bring you, Annie?"

▼

"Personal things," I mumble. "I could use some advice."

"Oh?" His bushy white eyebrows rise a bit.

"Actually, there are *two* things bothering me, Grandpa."

"Well — it's been some time since anyone came this way for that sort of help. Once your hair turns white and your body slows up, people begin to treat you like you have a feeble mind. Or Alzheimer's." He smiles bitterly. "Some of them even *yell* into my ear. I can't breathe so well, but my ears work just fine."

"Grandpa," I begin to protest, but he goes right on.

"You know, Annie, I have real sharp hearing. But in this plastic USA, old means worn out, obsolete. Discarded. I'm not talking about you guys — my family — you haven't discarded me. It's just that — my judgment isn't worth as much these days. I'm not called on to help make decisions for anyone.

"Now, if I'd been born in China, I'd grow wiser as I grew older. That's the way folks would feel. Here, I grow more foolish. Wouldn't this Trevor face have been something else in China? They'd respect my craft, too. They really appreciate fine handwork there." His eyes look up and out the window, as if he's seeing China.

Suddenly, he sits up straight and eyes me sharply. "I'm talking such nonsense, you'll really believe I'm round the bend."

"*I'm* a relative, Grandpa, and *I'm* here for advice."

"You always were a good kid. And very loyal. Okay,

out with it, girl. What have you done?" His words are tart, but his face is receptive. He's ready to listen.

The coward in me makes me put off the harder problem. "This first thing is sort of private. It's Kate's worry, really. But she didn't send me. She'd be sore if she knew I was talking about her."

Grandpa waves his hand impatiently. "It's our secret."

"She's miserable, Grandpa. She wants to get married, and Charlie won't hear about it until they've saved the down payment on a house. He puts in all the overtime he can and she works really hard and they are saving, but at night, she cries in her sleep. I talked to Mom and Dad, but they say it's not their place to interfere. I think someone has to. Why should Kate cry? Why shouldn't they get married and live together now — and save their money together? It could be years more."

"That's a hard call, Annie. Your parents are probably right. If they interfered, it wouldn't be taken well. If they had piles of money and could give the kids a hand, that would be different. No grown-up child wants parents to tell them what to do. You don't even like them to tell you what to do and you're only fourteen."

"Almost fifteen."

"Almost doesn't count because when you were almost born, you weren't here yet." Grandpa is proud of his logic.

"So Kate has to keep on waiting indefinitely — and crying. Because she and Charlie are nowhere near having a down payment. They'd need to win the lottery, which is hard because they won't even waste money on tickets." I had secretly bought several for them, but I'd never won a thing.

"That's sensible of them. You know what the odds are?" He knocks out the contents of his pipe into the big iron ashtray. "Let me think about this one, Annie. I don't believe I'm going to come up with anything, but I'd like to worry it a little. What else is on your mind?"

"Well — this one — you're going to think I'm crazy," I begin nervously.

"I've thought so off and on for a good long while," he teases. "Ever since I heard that music you listen to — those jabbering cassettes — "

"Grandpa, this is serious."

He rubs his thighs with the flats of his hands. "Serious at fourteen is different from serious at seventy." But he gives me his full attention.

I take a deep breath, then I exhale. I straighten my shoulders. And I begin. "I hate my nose — "

"Till now I thought my hearing was perfect." He moves his head forward a little, his brow wrinkled. "You *what*?"

"I hate my nose, Grandpa. I think it's ugly, and I'm considering having an operation."

Grandpa starts to laugh. He sits there on that bench, his body shaking. "I've heard a lot of peculiar things in my time, but that's the biggest cockamamie idea I ever heard."

"Daddy said you would say that."

"And what was his feeling on the subject?"

"The same as yours."

▼

"Good man. Sensible. I raised him right." He chews on his lower lip, holding back laughter. "I'm sorry," he says, "but, Annie, you don't know what you're talking about. You are a beautiful girl!"

I am a miserable girl. "Grandpa, my nose is wrong for my face. It has this bump on it."

"My nose has a bump on it, too." He touches it with his fingers. "So what?"

"Well, the bump bothers me. I think about it a lot. I'd really like to have a small, straight nose."

Grandpa is silent for a bit. "I'm an old man," he starts softly, "and I've heard a lot of strange things, but I've never heard the likes of this. Your nose is very much like mine, Annie. Are you saying I have an ugly nose?"

There it is, just as I had expected. Plain speaking.

"No. That is — on a man's face, it's not too bad. It's rugged. But I have a small face with smaller features. There's just too much nose."

"God made us this way."

"God made me with tonsils and an appendix, too. Both had to go."

"There were reasons. The tonsils were infected. The appendix you didn't need — you not being a ruminant — and it was causing trouble. Your nose does its job for you. It works fine."

"But it makes me feel ugly."

"This is all a lot of fuss over nothing," Grandpa says impatiently. "Teenagers overreact. You'll forget about the bump on your nose in a little while. More important things will occupy your mind. Much more important things."

▼

These words were almost exactly the same ones that Dee's mother has taken to saying about Dee's glasses lately. It seems impossible to tell adults how much the way we look means to us. They have all forgotten.

"No, Grandpa. I won't forget about it. It bothers me too much."

"It's sheer vanity." Getting up, he begins to walk about restlessly. "It's a lucky thing that you don't have the money to mutilate yourself. You're suffering from an obsession."

"I'm going to work extra hours and try to save up for an operation."

He comes over and puts his hands on my shoulders. "Don't do it, Annie. Don't go through pain and let them change your face for some newfangled style. You're a lovely girl as you are."

I get up. "I haven't made up my mind yet, Grandpa, but I'm heading that way. I have to think about it some more. I just wanted you to know that I was considering it."

"The idea makes me sick."

"Will you try to see it from my point of view, Grandpa? Can we talk about it again?"

"No," he says severely. "I know how I feel about it, and I am not going to change my mind. This is the first and the last conversation on this topic." He begins to cough. It takes a few minutes before he can finish what he's saying. "Forget it, Annie. It's a foolish idea."

He is having trouble with his breathing. We have talked too much.

▼

When he can, he starts once more. "I'd never be able to look at you — afterward — without thinking — " He has to pause, to rest and catch his breath, but he puts out a hand to hold me where I'm standing. "Vanity, vanity — " he starts, but he doesn't need to finish. He motions for me to go. "I'm okay," he reassures me. "I need to be quiet awhile."

I walk home in absolute misery.

NINE

Kate and I are sorting and folding the laundry still warm from the dryer. I do the socks, underwear, and the less-demanding stuff. Kate is terrific at folding shirts, blouses, and dresses. It's a weekly chore, and we have it down to a speedy system. We're out to break the Guinness record for the least time spent on laundry. Especially me. We are about halfway through when I ask my question.

"Kate, why don't you and Charlie just go ahead and get married and live in a small apartment while you're saving for a house? It wouldn't cost much more than now because you're both contributing for household expenses. You could even get married and live here."

Kate smiles. "You know how many times we've had this conversation over the laundry?"

"A few."

▼

"Fifty. A hundred. Maybe more."

"That's 'cause I still can't understand why you don't get married. If it were me — "

Kate's expression is serious. "Actually, *I* would. But Charlie can't. His childhood was such a nightmare of being poor and crowded in, one on top of the other, a baby a year coming into a family where there was no money and no space to breathe in. He just can't risk it again."

I shake my head as I try to match navy socks according to the weave. No easy job. My father is addicted to navy socks; if he bought a dozen pair of the same kind, then sorting would be a breeze. But, no, he buys single pairs that are great bargains and are slightly different. And he's got an eagle eye. If it were up to me, any navy matches any other navy. I'd even match it with black in a pinch. (Many days I purposely wear mismatched socks for style. Today I am wearing one fuschia and one yellow.) Anyway — who ever sees men's socks? Snakes, cats, caterpillars; creatures low on the ground, that's who.

So far, I haven't convinced Daddy.

I move way over to the window. Direct sunlight is great for sock-sorting. I pair and pile the socks against the sides of the half-filled laundry basket. "It would be different for you two," I say. "You're so much in love, and you're so sensible."

"Annie, it's a kind of permanent damage that Charlie suffered. I can tell him a million times that it would be different, but he remembers what it was like. He just can't bring himself to take the chance."

"So you have to wait and wait. I don't know if I'd be nice enough to do that for anyone."

"When you love someone, it isn't a question of nice enough. It's what you have to do."

"I think I'd try to talk him into seeing things my way. I *know* I'd try."

Kate sighs. "Don't you think I've done that? It only depresses him, and then we fight. There are some memories people can't overcome, Annie. What happens to us when we're little kids stays with us. Charlie is obsessed on the subject of neat closets and dresser drawers and having enough room to put things away. He can't help it."

Well, I certainly understand being obsessed. Still, it seems to me there should be some way out for them. "How long are you going to wait?"

"Till we have the down payment or some miracle occurs. Whichever happens first." She smiles.

Carefully, I load the piles of neatly folded clothing into the basket. "I'll put this stuff away. You go read *Bride* magazine or something." (It's her constant companion.)

"Thanks, Annie. You're a good kid."

I'm on my way when she says softly from behind me, "He's worth waiting for, Annie. I hate it, but I want you to understand that — no matter how long it takes — Charlie is worth it to me."

Maybe it's this conversation that upsets her, or maybe it's just her own blues, but late at night I hear Kate again sobbing in her sleep. As I lie there listening to her suffering, I promise myself that I will

▼

69

do something about it. I am going to help Kate. I might not be thanked for it, but I have to try. That's what sisters are for.

Sunday morning, opportunity knocks. Sunday morning, opportunity practically breaks down the door. Kate is washing her hair, that long thick auburn mop that makes washing an hour's job. Good safety time for me.

Charlie is out in the driveway lying under his 1980 blue Pontiac, doing something to its insides. That car runs beautifully; Charlie keeps it as carefully as a rare Rolls. "It's a vintage car," he loves to tell people.

"Yeah," I always add, "but 1980 was a *ba-ad* year."

Our driveway is not the greatest location for a private conversation, but he is trapped down under so he can't walk away.

I like Charlie. We've been casual friends for years ever since he started coming over to see Kate. We kid a lot; I tease him mostly about his baby, the car, and he finds a whole bunch of things about me weird: my mismatched socks, my bright lipstick, my health-food job; my friend Dee, who he nearly ran over because she was without her glasses. He likes me, too, but that's probably because I never butted into his life. I'm just Kate's kid sister.

I kneel down next to his legs, which are all that are visible. "Hi, Charlie. Don't tell me the chariot is broken."

"Naah." His voice is muffled. "Come on under and have a look at what makes a sweet car run."

"No thanks. What are you doing?"

"Admiring her. I just gave her a tune-up so she'll stay perfect."

"Charlie, I came out specially to ask you something — private."

"Sure, kid. Anything."

"Why don't you and Kate get married right now?"

There was a sudden climate change; we were in the Frigid Zone. "That's none of your business."

"You said I could ask you anything."

"Anything except that." His hands grab the bumper so he can bolster himself and slide out from under. Mr. All-American face — gray eyes, snub nose, sandy hair — is glaring up at me as I, kneeling, stare down.

"I think you two should get married and save your money for the house afterward."

"Oh, yeah? Anyone ask for this mature fourteen-year-old's advice?"

"I'm almost fifteen."

"Wow! You're ready to write the 'Dear Abby' column."

I let it pass. "Don't take it that way, Charlie. I just wanted to tell you on my own. Kate is dying to get married."

"What a surprise! Kiddo, I'm dying to get married, too."

"Well, then — "

He sat up right beside me so we were eye-to-eye. His eyes were slate now, clouded with anger. "Well, then, busybody, we'll get married when we have the money to get our own place. A decent place. Nobody's crowded, crummy, rented, roachy apartment. Our own house!"

"Charlie, that will take so long."

"We're working on it, kid, saving every extra penny. We're coming along. We're doing the best we can."

I could see he was really agitated and angry with me, but I couldn't erase what I'd started. I put my hand on his arm. "Charlie, she cries in her sleep almost every night."

"Who says?"

"I say. I sleep in the same room. Remember?"

Digging a red bandanna handkerchief out of his jeans backpocket, he wipes his face. "Listen, Annie, you're a good kid, but you don't know what you're talking about. You could never understand what it's like to live crowded without any privacy at all, never to have a bed or even a drawer of your own. No place to do homework. No place to think. If we start out crowded — " He shakes his head.

"You could move into our house with Kate. I'd be glad to sleep on the living room couch. It's real comfortable."

He snorts at that. "I couldn't do that to you. I slept on the living room couch for the first fifteen years of my life. Till my older brothers moved out, and there was a bed for me. Every one of the springs in that couch was sharp as the point of a knife. And I had to be the last one to go to bed. You know what that means to an athlete who needs his sleep?"

"It wouldn't be the same, Charlie. I'd be glad to do it for you and Kate. I've already had all these years

▼

in a comfortable bed, so what's a little time on the couch? Besides, ours is foam rubber. No springs."

"No thanks, Annie. We're saving. With all my over-time money, we're going to make it soon. I hate for Kate to be crying; you know that. But it'll be worth it in the end. We'll have space and walk-in closets and drawers to put stuff away. We'll have a clean, modern kitchen with plenty of room to work in — and to hang out in the way a family should — and some of those machines that make living easy. We'll set the machines going, and then we'll sit and drink our coffee while they do their work. And if they break down, you-know-who will be right there to fix them. It'll be great."

"I wonder if it's worth waiting for."

"I don't wonder," Charlie says. "Not for a second. *I* know! It's paradise, USA."

I'm nervous that Kate will be along any minute, and she'll feel I went behind her back. I didn't mean it that way; I only wanted to help. "Will you, at least, think about it, Charlie?" I borrow a line from Mom. "Don't close your mind. I might even prefer the couch. In a way, it would be more private than shar-ing my room. I mean, no one else sleeps in the living room. Don't say no just because you're stubborn, or because I'm fifteen."

"You're fourteen."

"Closer to fifteen but, whatever — please consider it."

"Yeah," he says. "Okay, I'll try. Now let's drop it. Speaking of considering things, Kate tells me you are considering plastic surgery. Now that is one

▼
73

weird little idea. A girl with a nice face like yours, sitting around stewing about her nose."

"Charlie" — I stand up so I can command more dignity — "I am considering it, you're right. I've spent a lot of time viewing all sides of the subject — "

"Mostly in the mirror?" He's grinning.

"That, too. Anyway, I don't have a closed mind on the subject." Now I'm sore. How can he compare my thoughtful weighing of my problem with his stubborn pigheadedness? "How much time have you spent worrying about Kate and what this long delay means to her? Mostly, I bet, you think about your hard childhood and yourself. And how you're going to show everyone what a big shot you are with this house that you'll own."

Now he springs up. "I said let's drop it. Annie, just because you're young doesn't mean you can say anything that comes into your head. Words affect people. They can hurt a lot."

"I don't mean to hurt. I'm trying to get words to move you so you'll make my sister happy."

"As if that isn't what I want to do most."

"Then think about it, Charlie. Think LIVING ROOM COUCH!"

He shrugs. "All right, all right. I'll think — if I can do it without exploding. Meanwhile, you work on your own problem." He sticks out a greasy hand. "I know you meant well. Friends?"

I stand up on tiptoe and kiss his cheek. "In-laws first," I say. "Friends later."

He tilts his head in a kind of salute. "You Trevor

▼

women are something else. You all look so little and easy to push around. But that's a mistake. Listen, if you decide you want to see a plastic surgeon — just to talk to — I'll find you the best guy around. But take it from me, you got a nice face now."

"The nose needs a tune-up, Charlie," I say, "so it'll be in perfect running order. A vintage nose." I duck inside.

TEN

Saturday morning I get to YIN/YANG/YUMMY before eight in the morning. I usually work nine to five, but it's such a busy store they always need extra help. I figure I can easily add one early hour and one more at the end of the day, as long as the old fingers and hands hold out working the register, packing, or setting out stock on the shelves.

I check in with Mr. Buehler. He is sitting at his little desk, the eternal bottle of pure water on it. Mr. Buehler is on a quest for the best drinking water in the world. Today it is Bourassa Canadian Natural Pure Glacial Water. (Bob's joke is that he guzzles the costly stuff like water.)

"Have a drink," my boss urges. "It's absolutely pure." He is a dedicated man, a missionary in the Organic Foods Crusade. I take a drink. It's delicious.

"You're early," he says, checking the work sched-

▼

ule. "I have you down for nine o'clock."

I explain about wanting to work extra hours. "Sure," he agrees. "I can use you as much as you want to work."

"Mr. Buehler," I start a little uncertainly, "my science teacher is looking for a speaker to talk about alternative ideas in food and health. I recommended you."

"You're putting me on," he laughs. "I know what high school teachers are like. They read the textbook, staying one step ahead of the class. Then they make up a list of ten inconsequential questions on every chapter."

He must have had Mr. Collins for Shakespeare.

"No. Ms. Campion — this teacher — is not like that. She's an environmentalist, and she's teaching this new Living course — orientation for the world after high school. She's really unusual. And interesting."

Mr. Buehler is alerted. "How old is she?"

"Oh, maybe close to thirty. I'm not sure."

"Tell me more," he says, pouring me another glass of pure water. To talk to Mr. Buehler for ten minutes, you need to be a sponge. I sip cautiously. The more I tell him about the great Ms. C, the more interested he gets.

"Sure, I'll come and talk," he says. "Give her my card and tell her to call me and we'll make arrangements." He takes out his stash of cards on recycled, wheat-colored parchment, and hands me a bunch (just to be safe, in case I misplace four or five). Mr. Buehler is definitely interested, and I don't think it's

Mr. Buehler the Organic Missionary; I think it's Mr. Buehler the Man!

The whole thing bends my mind. Till this invitation to class, I have always thought of him as past such things. I guess that's the way I think about most older people, though he's not really *that* old. Maybe it's because he eats tons of wakame (Japanese seaweed) in his Amaranth Flakes (protein cereal), and the rest of his diet seems to be mostly brown rice and chick-peas and lentils, arame and nori (more Japanese seaweed), and shitake mushrooms at fourteen dollars a pound. Or maybe it's because he looks so much like Woody Allen and has a personality like him, too — only not as funny.

"Listen," he says, "your boyfriend is here. Been here since late last night, working on stock. I have him out in produce now, sorting. Say" — he rears back on his chair, pretending to eye me suspiciously — "you two cooking up some plot to take over YIN/YANG/YUMMY?" He's amused by his joke.

"Sure, Mr. Buehler. The Tofu Connection. That's us."

That breaks him up. "All right, kid. You can run back and say hello to him before you start work. But, remember, no hanky-panky back there."

Mr. Buehler lives with the constant fear that there will be a sex orgy among the wilted lettuce and endive and kiwi fruit and avocados, and that his outpost of natural foods and organically grown vegetables will be raided by the police. Some of the kids love to tease him by flirting wildly in passing, but the store is so busy, there is hardly time to eye one another, much less make out.

I once asked him, "Do you think all these health foods are helping you, Mr. Buehler? I mean like you're so tense."

"You should have seen me before, Annie. Ten years ago I was a smoker, a drug-user, and a drunk. I *know* this diet, this whole new way of life, helps me. Helps? It keeps me alive!"

This was stunning news. Eccentric Mr. Buehler has this incredible history? *Mr. Buehler?* You really can't tell about people.

Both security guards come rushing up at once. Not even nine o'clock in the morning and already crises: an angry housewife has been overcharged fifty-three cents for swordfish steaks at the fish counter, and the Macadamia Nut Mystery has been solved!

The swordfish lady gets a refund and an apology. Then Mr. Buehler turns to the big one. For weeks, someone has been scooping quantities of our expensive macadamia nuts from the jar, but not getting them weighed or paying for them. Some days, when no register rings up the nuts, pounds of them are gone. The mystery was driving Mr. Buehler mad. Now, the excited security guard explains, they've caught the thief. The delivery man who brings the whole-grain breads has been filling his pockets and eating the nuts while he shelves the bread. His pocket apparently tore this morning as he reached up high, munching away, so he began to dribble tell-tale macadamia nuts. Our ace guard stalked him until he went from the bread shelves back to the jar for a refill. There he was nabbed.

The checkers are detaining him up front. "The guy says he has a macadamia nut deficiency," the bewildered guard says.

"Then he can buy them like everyone else." Mr. Buehler hurries off to dispense justice.

I have never known him to turn in a shoplifter. He talks very tough, then he lets them go. So, if the Macadamia Nut Marauder pleads macrobiotics and yin and yang, Mr. Buehler will surely let him go. The people who patronize our store are like a secret society with their own language and customs. *Additives* is the dirtiest word ever spoken. They despise paper diapers. They hate plastic. (Grandpa would approve.) They need to know what's biodegradable. They choose their detergents so carefully, you'd think it was medicine they were buying. We give a five cents-per-bag credit to shoppers who bring their own shopping bags. Most of our customers collect.

While I'm slipping into the stiff, wheat-colored uniform, I worry about why Bob has been here since last night. I stick the drab matching bow in my hair — some organic lunatic has designed these outfits for maximum discomfort and ugliness — and I grab a work-coat to wrap around me while I go look for Bob out back. The air-conditioning is always crazy there.

He is sitting on a bench in the frigid, silent, produce-storage room, sorting strawberries, getting rid of the squashy old rotten ones as he fills wooden-slatted pound containers with ripe young berries. He

▼

looks absolutely terrible, his eyes sunken in shadows. He is shivering. I slip out of the work-coat and drape it over his shoulders, and then I kiss him on the cheek. "Put your arms into the sleeves," I order. "You're freezing."

He puts the coat on and buttons it up. "Boy, that feels good." He rubs his hands and stamps his feet. "I *was* freezing and I didn't even realize it."

"How come you're here?"

He doesn't want to talk about it.

"Bob — what happened?"

"Don't ask."

"I already asked."

He shakes his head.

"Bob — "

"You can guess."

"Your father."

"Got it on the very first try. The lady wins a strawberry. A double!" He gives me a luscious twin-berry.

"What happened?"

"We had a fight. It doesn't matter what it was about, does it? Pritchitt Senior and Pritchitt Junior went at it again."

"I'm sorry, Bob."

"Yeah. Me, too."

"Tell me about it. You'll feel better."

"I doubt that."

"Try it. You've been sitting here all night, alone, in the cold. Talk to me." I rub his cheek. "I care about you."

He begins to talk, but keeps sorting the berries mechanically as he talks so he won't have to look at

▼

me. "He came home loaded last night. Instead of just falling into bed, he suddenly began turning the house upside down, looking for the book Raymond made such a fuss over. He really had to search it out because I never leave anything of value where he can get his hands on it."

"You took it back to the library?" I'm praying that he did.

"No such luck." Bob pops a mashed berry into the discards savagely. "He found it, all right, and I wanted to go take it away from him, but my mother locked me in their bedroom and wouldn't let me out."

"Why did he want it?"

"Guess. He's a better shredder than the CIA ever had." Bob's eyes are glassy. He is barely holding back tears.

I dig out a tissue for him.

"It was such a beautiful book," he mourns, "and he just stumbled around drunkenly, making garbage out of it and strewing it all around like confetti. Like he makes garbage out of our lives. It's so hard to believe he's my father. While he's doing this, he keeps cursing the dean and Raymond and the school and me, calling me his little fairy picture snapper. He's an animal when he's drunk."

I can't think of anything to say.

"My mother says it's a sickness, and I should forgive him. But I don't. I don't!"

I stroke his arm. "Sh." Someone could come in any minute. I don't want Bob embarrassed. "What happened after he tore up the book?"

"He just flopped down on the floor with a beer and

sat there muttering to himself and giggling. Crazy giggling. Finally, my mother let me out so she could get him into bed. Then I ran over here."

I just keep stroking. I don't know what to say.

"I'll have to tell the library I lost the book and pay for it. It must be thirty dollars, at least. I don't mind that as much as I mind that he destroyed a beautiful thing for nothing. Maybe because it was beautiful." Bob flings a handful of rotten strawberries away. "I have to get out," he whispers. "Annie, I have to get away."

"I know it's terrible," I say softly, "but it's just a couple of months till graduation. You've held on for so long. If you could just hold on a little longer, till you get your diploma — it's your ticket to a better life." I am simply repeating what I have heard all my life. In my family, graduation from high school is about as important for survival as oxygen.

Bob's eyes are bleak. "Annie, I've been trying. I don't open my mouth to him. I tiptoe in the house. But" — his voice catches — "I may not be able to make it. He's getting worse as I get closer to graduating. I don't think he wants me to graduate. How would you feel about a boyfriend who's a dropout?"

Lucky that Mr. Buehler has to handle the Macadamia Nut Maniac up front. I break my word to the boss. In my mind, it's justifiable hanky-panky. I put my arms around Bob and hold him tight. While I am holding him, I remember what Kate said about Charlie. No matter how long she has to wait, Charlie is worth it to her. I am beginning to understand that better.

▼

"Bob, you know you don't have to ask that. You're you — with or without the diploma — one of the smartest and nicest people I know."

"And a great photographer as well?" He is beginning to climb up out of his despair.

"That goes without saying." I kiss him lightly.

"Say it anyway."

"And a great photographer as well. In fact, could you take a few shots of me during the lunch break?"

"Sure. Any special reason?"

"I'll explain later. If I don't get my cash drawer and go up front right now, Mr. Buehler will suffer an anxiety attack."

Bob manages a weak smile. "Okay. Lunchtime pictures means you in your native costume." He is looking at the monster, baggy uniform. "I have seen you look classier."

"Today I need *bad* pictures. The worst."

"Oh?" I'm already heading out, so he can't question me. "In that case, you're perfectly dressed."

I blow him a kiss and head for check-out.

Lunch break.

We buy chestnut croquettes and Cranapple juice. We became addicted to the croquettes when we were demonstrating how to make them, and we love them for sentimental reasons as well. We wander into the small park that adjoins the store. Bob's camera bag looks heavy on his shoulder.

"Which camera do you have today?"

"Both. I'm not going to leave them where he can get his hands on them."

"Good thinking."

"I'm going to sleep with them from now on."

"You could leave them at my house."

"Thanks. But then I wouldn't have them on hand. I never know when a great picture suddenly presents itself."

We sit on a wrought-iron bench in the sunlight, eating our healthful lunches and tossing occasional crumbs at the pigeons. They are wild for chestnut-croquette crumbs. It's peaceful here away from the frantic Saturday shoppers.

"Now what's this business about bad pictures, Annie?"

"I need three or four Polaroid shots of my face. Profile or full-face, but not pretty. Realistic."

"How come? You never take profile shots."

"I want to use them for propaganda."

"I must be dense from lack of sleep. Spell it out."

"I have to talk my father and my grandfather — if that's possible — into seeing that I need a nose repair job. They both insist I'm pretty, that I have the Trevor family nose, which is nothing to worry about. I want them to *really* see my nose."

"That's crazy. A photographer can make you ugly or beautiful. It has very little to do with you, actually. You are asking me to make you ugly. I don't think I want to do that."

"Don't you want to help me?"

"Sure. But photography is an art. I don't take distorted pictures on purpose. I like to take shots where you come out lovely." He takes my hand. "That's the way I think of you."

▼

I pull my hand free. "I just want you to take some profile shots. No distortions. No exaggerations or fake anything." I am very upset with him. "Don't you understand? The nose is ugly. It's there. Can't you just take straight, honest shots and give them to me?"

He studies me, considering what I've asked. It would not be a big thing to ask of anyone else. But Bob is so hung up on his photography, it's almost a holy art.

"Will you take the pictures for me, or do I have to go to the photography store in the mall? Because that's what I'll do. I have to do this, Bob. I *have* to. I can't live with this nose!"

"I guess I can take some straight shots of you: full-face and profile" — he says at last — "and they won't be gently angled, so you can use them for your prop-aganda. They're not going to be pictures I'm proud of. I like your nose. I don't believe you need an operation."

"I believe it enough for both of us."

He takes out his camera and gets it ready and then he poses me for the first profile pictures of my life.

The Polaroid does not lie. In minutes we have evidence of my need for surgery. My nose — to me — is grotesque.

"Thanks," I tell him. "I really appreciate this."

"Now I get to take some pretty ones," he says, and he goes about it happily using both the Polaroid and the Nikon. There's no question about it; the photographer transforms the subject. Even in the incredibly ugly, oatmeal-colored, stiff YIN/YANG/YUMMY clothing, I look terrific on the later shots.

▼

While Bob is switching cameras, a dog walker comes by, fussing at his wonderfully fat basset hound. "*Raymond*, when I say heel, you'd better heel!" he scolds.

"Please, sir," Bob stops him, "would you take a picture of both of us? We'd love to have your dog, Raymond, in it, too."

"I'd be glad to. But Raymond doesn't deserve it. He's a naughty dog!"

He snaps an absolutely stunning shot of the two of us, kneeling, with Raymond in the middle. It's my favorite picture in the whole world, the two of us in those cartoon-character droopy uniforms, laughing in the sunlight with that droopy-looking dog in between.

Bob says that the dog looks like the world's greatest expert on *checks and balances*.

ELEVEN

On Buehler-in-the-School day, I wear my good black turtleneck shirt, my Gap jeans, and my best mismatched socks, one white one black, in his honor. Squeezing through the crowd on the stairs coming up from phys ed, I try to be first in the classroom where Living meets, but by the time I get there the front row is already filled with the usual flakes, Fats Russell and his friends. They really must have hotfooted it out of gym.

"Hey, Bump," Fats greets me, "is it true that health foods increase a man's sex drive?"

"*Sex* drive? Why're you asking, Fats? You don't even have a learner's permit yet."

That gets catcalls and whistles. "Way to go, Bump," some rat stomps applause. Fats's face reddens, but he laughs to show he doesn't mind. I laugh, too. I have learned how.

"Fats is dreamin' of five-on-the-floor." His buddy Mike wiggles bent fingers madly. "You know, hand clu-utch!" Mike gasps and pants dramatically, his idea of a paroxysm of sex. It sounds like a bad asthma attack.

"Anyone here know CPR?" I ask, and move to take a seat. Their lunatic mood worries me. Mr. Buehler is going to take a lot of abuse. Since inviting him was my idea, I'm sort of responsible.

Dee arrives. She is wearing a scoop-necked white cotton knit that earns her whistles from the goon section. Girls with nice breasts make them nervous. The boys our age have a lot of trouble getting used to *our* body changes, never mind their own. Dee is cool. All they are to her is a blur, anyway. She sits near me. "I'm looking forward to this, Annie. They say certain foods will strengthen people's eyes. You think this guy will know about them?"

"He might. He can at least tell you where you can find out. A quarter says he's going to hand out a reading list."

"In this crowd? You and I will probably be the only takers." She begins to unpack her gear: first her eyeglasses, and then her pastel marker for shading important notes, and her Eraser Mate pen, and her spiral notebook that says RUTGERS UNIVERSITY. Her father works in New Brunswick and buys her supplies there. Guess who comes in making sure everyone sees *her* notebooks — she carries them covers out — which say YALE? Vickie One-Upham. "YALE," her blue sweatshirt screams at us.

"Your father works in New Haven?" I ask as she passes. Does she really think we believe any college man, even from NERD UNIVERSITY, would hang out with her?

Dee has her desk neatly organized. She is a shrewd note taker; she knows exactly what cue words and phrases to take down, and what to underline, and what to shade in pastel because it's critical. When we study together, we use her notes more than mine, but she's teaching me how to listen and sort the stuff out. It takes concentration.

Ms. Campion, in a classy denim dress hinged together with big brass Save-the-Whales buttons (shaped like whales), comes in with our guest. Can it be? Surely it can't. Yet — yes! It is! Grungy Mr. Buehler, but today he is Mr. America. He is wearing a navy blazer and gray slacks, a pale blue button-down shirt, and an amazing white tie with big red polka dots on it. I have never seen him in anything but the tacky work-clothes we all wear in the store. Today he looks positively Yuppie. This impression is further supported by the stylish attaché case in his hand. Mr. Buehler, whom I've only seen carrying grocery bags.

Ms. Campion is all smiles, glowing. "Our guest today is Cal Buehler, a graduate of Rutgers (Yeah Dee! The right notebooks!), Class of 1974, who owns and operates YIN/YANG/YUMMY, the natural-food store in the mall. He has come to tell us a little about nontraditional diet."

Immediately, Fats's hand shoots up, and before Ms. Campion can call on him, he is into his question. "Is it true that health foods increase a man's sex drive?"

"I'd like to say *yes* and make you all lifelong customers," Mr. Buehler says to the front-row lineup of clowns, "but I have to admit that I doubt it. I believe that if you eat properly, it improves your general health and a healthier person is a sexier person."

Fats's hand rises again.

"Let's hold the questions, William, till the end," Ms. Campion suggests. Her voice says *no fooling around*.

Casually, Mr. Buehler sits down on the front desk and hikes his gray flannels up so he's comfortable. "I'm not here to show you THE WAY," he begins, "or even to give you a miracle-cure testimonial. I'm just going to tell you a little about myself and what happened to me, and how I came to macrobiotics." He goes to write it on the board:

> macro = great
> biotics = rejuvenation (life)

"I grew up in a little Jersey town like you guys. When I was a kid, my parents made decisions for me. I had no choice. In high school and afterwards, when I moved away from home, I let my peers make the decisions for the way I lived. I never really controlled my own life. I went along for years doing whatever my friends did. Alcohol. Junk food. Pot. Cocaine. Pills to make me high and pills to take me down. You name it, I tried it.

"I didn't have a breakdown or any kind of big Hollywood-type crisis. I just experienced slow burn-out. I was always depressed. I realized that I wasn't going anywhere with my life, and I had never even had a shot at it.

"So — I began looking around. There were a lot of choices out there, a lot of strange groups. All looking for loners. These days people don't talk about them much, but they're still out there ready to suck you in."

He does a little describing of the way cults latch on to a person and use sleep-deprivation and brain-washing to chew up the mind. It's scary.

"I read a lot, and I began to talk to people whose style I liked. And, finally, I worked out a way of life — and diet — that's right for me. And I'm much happier.

"I'm not here to recruit anyone. Too many years of my own life were co-opted. My way derives very loosely from Taoism" — he wrote the word on the board — "an ancient Chinese philosophy that explains the world in terms of opposites. Taoists try to keep conflicting forces in balance. I've brought you reading lists on Taoism and macrobiotics."

▼

The words *reading list* in Edison High School trigger an automatic response from the class — a grumble. He got his automatic grumble.

"Taking the lists is completely up to you. I'll distribute them later. In Taoism, balance is the key word."

Dee writes *Balance*, and then runs her pink marker over it.

"Food is delightful for all the usual reasons, but it serves one other basic function: It can prevent diseases and make us healthy. Along with herbs, it can restore health to any ailing body.

"Taoists divide food into five categories based on taste. Each category nourishes a certain body organ, as well as the physical functions and feelings that relate to that organ." He stops and looks around. "Too technical for you? Shall I go on?"

"Yes, yes. Go on." A lot of people urge him. Even the front row is interested.

"Bitter foods affect the heart and small intestines; salty foods, the kidneys and bladder; sweet foods, the spleen, pancreas, and stomach; sour foods, the liver and gallbladder; and hot, spicy foods, the lungs and large intestines."

"Thinking about all that stuff takes the fun out of eating," Fats complains.

"Not really. I like my food to be attractive and delicious. And I do love to eat. But I know what the food I eat does for me. I'm not fanatic. In company I don't make a big fuss. I try to fit in."

▼

"Like — what is a balanced meal for you people?"
Ms. Yale asks.

Not a blink indicates that Mr. Buehler is unaccustomed to being addressed as *you people*.

"Well," he says, "I'm glad you asked. I had a terrific dinner last night: brown rice cooked with sesame oil, garlic, ginger, scallions, and a bit of vinegar. And some spinach topped with an egg and an avocado."

This oddball menu prods the class into groans and whispers.

"Gross," Vickie shudders. "That would kill me." She makes an unbeautiful retching noise.

"What did you have for dinner last night?" Mr. Buehler asks her.

Pigs' ears, snakes' hearts, and poison ivy are my idea of a balanced diet for her.

"Filet mignon, French fries, onion rings."

Up front, Fats moans with pleasure. "Now you're talking food."

"We're even," Mr. Buehler tells her, "because as a regular diet, that food would kill me. And I believe it is dangerous for you" — his eyes move to Fats — "and for you, too."

Vickie writhes at being paired with Fats.

I love it.

Ms. Campion gets up and moves to stand next to our speaker. "Our time is almost up. Please tell us why you named your store YIN/YANG/YUMMY."

"The terms are, again, Chinese, and the answer is balance. YIN is the dark, passive, female cosmic element. YANG is the bright, active, male cosmic element. They are opposites but also complementary. Their interaction influences our destinies. YUMMY, is, of course, self-explanatory."

Ms. Campion looks rather doubtful about the dark, passive, female cosmic element.

"More modern definitions are YIN is acidity, and YANG alkalinity," Mr. Buehler adds.

Students outside in the hall are jiggling the doorknob like crazy; the next class wants in.

Hurriedly, Mr. Buehler sets his attaché case on the desk. "On your way out, if you like, pick up some reading lists and some healthful sweets." He snaps open the lock and under the pile of lists are Granola Bars, Tofu Chocolate-covered Mints, Sugarless Cocoa Caramel Bars, Tofu Chocolate-covered Raisins. "I brought a small sampling of candy that is really *good* for you. Help yourselves."

Kids crowd around picking up candy bars, and, surprisingly, lists.

Filet mignon, French fries, and onion rings moves to the door dramatically as if she can't get out fast enough. Good riddance.

Fats crams a Cocoa Caramel Bar in his mouth. "Not totally bad for something that's good for you," he concedes. He takes three more, but no reading list.

"Thanks, Mr. Buehler," I say, along with many of the others. I wait to walk him out, but he is waiting for Ms. Campion. Dee and I stand to one side. Dee whispers to me, "She's more Yang than she should be, but maybe they can work it out. Annie, you've made a match."

"First time I ever tried it, and it's fun." I can't wait to tell Bob. Sushi met bean sprout! Maybe we achieved a cosmic balance. *Plej fenomenega!* as Monsieur Simon says. And my mother says it, too, all the time. She says it beats *awesome* by a mile.

TWELVE

I carry the bad Polaroid pictures around in an envelope in my pocket. I'm a nut case; twenty times a day I secretly take them out and look at them and shudder. One part of me is bold and wants to move swiftly. The other part of me is holding back because I am scared to death.

Bold Annie gets Kate to find out from Charlie who the best plastic surgeon affiliated with the hospital is, and then to make an appointment with him in his private office for a first consultation (no commitment). The magician's name: Dr. Ricci.

Scared Annie trembles as she sits around worrying about what Daddy and Grandpa will say when they hear about it.

I can't keep stalling forever. I have to do something about them, something that will change their minds. First, I have to make the pitch to Daddy myself. It

▼

wasn't fair to put it on Mom, to let her do the arguing for me, particularly because she doesn't feel the shape of my nose is a life-and-death question. Because I do feel that way, I figure I can be more persuasive. And then I have these pictures as hard evidence.

"Daddy," I start one night as we two are alone in the living room and Mom is off in the kitchen. "I know Mom talked to you about my nose and the operation I'm thinking of, and I know you were against it. Have you thought about it, and — maybe — changed your mind?"

"I have thought about it, but I haven't changed my mind. The answer is still no. No operation. Your nose stays as it is. It's the classic Trevor nose. It's been passed along for generations. No one ever complained about it before."

"But it makes me unhappy."

"It shouldn't."

"You can't tell a person that something that bothers her shouldn't bother her."

"I am telling you exactly that. This preoccupation with your nose will pass away. You'll forget about it."

"You spent so much money getting my teeth straightened. Why should you object to me having a bump removed from my nose?"

"Because Nature made you that way. That's you."

"Aren't my teeth me, too?"

He is getting annoyed with me. "Orthodontia is superficial, correcting small flaws. There's no cutting involved, no blood."

"Daddy, please don't get mad. Don't you mind that you're losing your hair? Doesn't it make you unhappy?"

He is taken aback, but he knows I didn't say it to put him down. "Well, my baldness doesn't make me jump for joy."

"It bothers you?"

"I wouldn't say *bother*. While I'm not ready to feature my head on the cover of *People*, I manage not to suffer too much."

"But you suffer a little, Daddy?"

"Very little."

"Yet you won't do anything about it."

"You mean will I wear a toupee or let them paste hair on me or fertilize my scalp with chemicals? No, I will not."

"You think that makes you a better person than the people who get these things done to them?"

"I don't know about them. If they need crutches, let them have their crutches. I manage."

"But I'm not even fifteen years old. I have a very long time to live with a nose I don't like. I just want to be pretty."

"You are pretty." He's exasperated with me. "You have a boyfriend. You're not lonely. You're smart and you do well in school. I don't understand what ails you. Never, I swear it, never have I given one single thought to your nose."

"I think about it constantly."

He shakes his head. "The whole world is trying to make itself over into what it isn't. You look at the TV ads and the newspapers and magazines. Everybody hates himself, I guess, because they're all trying to be someone else, to look different, and act different, and smell different. No matter what color their hair is, they want to change it. Skinny is dying to be fat, and fat wants only to be skinny. Even fingernails. The young women in my office paste claws on their fingernails so their hands are practically useless. And you're telling me this is the race you want to enter and run in."

"Daddy, did you know that I wanted to be a junior cheerleader? Because Kate was so beautiful in that short flared maroon skirt and white sweater and white boots with the gold tassels — and Charlie fell in love with her when he played football for Edison — I dreamed about doing it, too."

"You never told us."

"It was a private dream." I had sworn to myself never to tell anyone. "When I was finally eligible, I went to the tryouts. I had worked out a clever cheer and I practiced it a million times in the bathroom. When I got to the gym, I sat in the back of the bleachers and I watched Miss Duncan, the gym teacher, audition the candidates. My cheer was really good — I could tell that from listening to the others — but after a while I knew I wouldn't make it. I wasn't pretty enough. Miss Duncan paid particular attention to the cute, bouncy girls with the movie star faces. She really wasn't interested in clever cheers. Or in the heavy or skinny girls who came to try out. I could see how she dismissed them, politely but quickly. That's the way she would treat a girl with a klunky nose. I cut out of there fast."

"You didn't try out?"

"She wouldn't have picked me."

"You'll never know."

"I know."

"You gave in to fear, Annie," he said sadly. "You're pretty enough naturally, just as you are. I think you're beautiful."

I finger the profile shots in my pocket, ready to offer irrefutable proof.

He smiles at me. "You have the best of your mother and me. I've always been very proud of my girls."

I can't bring myself to take out the bad pictures. Not while he's being so sweet.

"No one in the office is prouder of his kids than I am. I carry snapshots of both of you and I show them at the drop of a hat."

"I know. That's because you're my father."

He sighs. "I'm against an operation, Annie. Besides the unnecessary danger that you would be facing — and surgery is always dangerous, don't let anyone kid you — the only thing in the world that's going to make you think you're beautiful is self-respect. All the cosmetics and operations can't possibly give you that."

"We're not talking about the same thing, Daddy. You are dealing with inner beauty. I am worried about my outer beauty."

The conversation ends there, and I kiss him good-night. There is nowhere we two can go.

* * *

▼

Whenever I make oatmeal-raisin cookies, or soda bread — my two specialties — I always take Grandpa a supply, so I am a frequent visitor at his house. Ever since our conversation about my nose, however, I respect his wishes and do not mention it. He probably thinks I've discarded the idea, like so many other of my teenage fancies, what he likes to call my scatterbrained ideas. (And he thinks *old people* don't get respect! Teenagers get nothing but abuse, some of it from old people.)

While I am forbidden to talk to him about my nose, no one said anything about writing. I am pretty good at getting my ideas down on paper. I work on the school newspaper, and English is my best subject.

So I spend one whole long night composing this carefully argued, reasonable, undeniable document for Grandpa. The great arguer of the American Revolution, Tom Paine: *"These are the times that try men's souls . . ."* would be mighty proud of me. I keep at it and do many drafts until I have it exactly as I want it. When I have a final rough draft, I kiss the paper with joy. I keep reading it over, then putting it down and walking away to get some distance from it, and then taking it up to read again. Every word is perfect. Shakespeare must have felt just the same way when he wrote "Ende" on a play.

I call Dee up and read it to her, and she is impressed.

"It's terrific," she says. "It would persuade a rock."

"How about my grandfather?"

She's not so sure. "Send it and see."

I begin to copy my letter carefully on clean paper.

▼

Dear Grandpa,

I know you don't want to talk about my getting a nose operation, so I thought I would write to you and tell you all about my reasons and the way I think. I want you to consider them because you are a reasonable and thoughtful person.

You are right about one thing. Getting my nose fixed has become a kind of obsession. I find I can't get it out of my mind entirely no matter what else I am doing. Nothing has ever possessed me this way before. It's a little frightening.

I have always believed what you told me from the time I was a little kid and we used to hang out together at the Bronx Zoo. That I should enjoy this blessed life that was given me, enjoy it and live it fully: read, learn, listen, and be aware.

That's the way I want to live, Grandpa, but I find that I can't while a part of me is ugly. It makes me miserable, and I think about it to the exclusion of other things. I am enclosing several pictures of my profile. I know you are a fair person and so I ask you to look at them and then decide whether or not that is an ugly nose that needs fixing.

Please try to see my side of it. Maybe it is very selfish and immature of me, but it is the way I am. I love you and Daddy so much, and both of you are so against this. I don't want to do something you'll hate. So I am writing this in hope that you will change your mind.

Your loving granddaughter,
Annie

Folding it carefully with the pictures inside, I address the envelope and carefully pack it up and seal it. I don't mail it immediately. I am waiting for exactly the right moment, for a good omen. For a sign!

THIRTEEN

As Kate and I enter Dr. Ricci's office, his stereo is softly beginning "I Feel Pretty," from *West Side Story*. We did the play in school last year; I was in the chorus and I love the song. "You think that's just for me, or does he play it all the time to cheer up customers?" I ask Kate.

"Wait and see."

We listen. The song is part of a medley.

"Coincidence," Kate says.

"The song began the minute I opened the door. It's a sign. An omen."

She laughs at me.

Charlie has set things up for this visit. "Dr. Ricci's the best in his field," Charlie says. "He drives a red Porsche convertible that's worth fifty thou easily. The man's good. And you don't have to worry; there is no charge for this consultation. I explained that you're not sure and you're just coming in to talk."

Charlie has been very sweet about all this, considering . . . I am grateful that he doesn't hold a grudge about my butting in and telling him to get married. (On the other hand, he's not practicing walking to "Here Comes the Bride" yet, either.)

I haven't eaten all day out of nervousness, but once I enter the clean light office and I hear the lucky music, I sense that somehow everything is going to be okay. On the low, gray-and-white marble table there are the usual piles of *Better Homes and Gardens*, a weirdo publication called *Forbes*, and at least a dozen *Rolling Stones*. First time in my life I ever saw *RS* roll into a doctor's office. The vibes are getting better by the minute. "What's this *Forbes* thing?" I ask Kate.

"A business magazine. Investment advice, interviews with guys who made it big. That kind of thing. The Forbes family, who publish it, are millionaires."

"Neat to be able to put your name on a magazine. What do you think, Kate? Could there be a magazine called *Trevor*?"

"Why not *Annie*? That's a catchy name."

I consider that idea. She's right. *Annie* is a kind of nice name for a magazine. Music reviews, interviews with top stars like Barbra, pages of stunning photos taken by Bob, glossy brown-rice and pure-water ads paid for by Mr. Buehler. Some fashion, maybe, and short stories and poems. Something to dream about.

"Ms. Trevor?" The nurse in the tiny reception area hands me a long questionnaire. "Please fill this out."

I like being *Ms. Trevor*. The quantity of questions startles me. I haven't brought any money with me. "I'm only here to consult," I say, surprised that my voice is shaking. "Nothing has been decided."

"I understand. This is information Dr. Ricci needs. It helps him evaluate your condition."

Evaluate my condition? He only has to look at me.

The sheet contains every possible question that can be asked of a living creature with a nose. Slowly, I begin to read and then to work my way down the list. Dr. Ricci needs to know, first of all, my name, age, sex, height, weight, and whether or not I have ever had any surgery. Reasonable questions. Relevant.

I am a veteran of surgery. I list tonsillectomy and appendectomy.

Did I ever have plastic surgery previously?

Dumb question. Would anyone with a nose like mine have other work done first?

Then the questions begin to concentrate on *le nez*.

Has it ever been injured? When? Details and treatment.

How do I breathe, easily or with difficulty?

How frequently do I get colds?

Do I have a deviated septum?

Do I have nasal polyps? (I certainly hope not.) Sinusitis? Frequent nosebleeds?

As I sit there answering these gross questions, it occurs to me that Grandpa is right about my nose doing its job. Other noses must do all these awful things, but my nose behaves. It never makes any trouble. It just doesn't look good.

▼

Suddenly, Dr. Ricci is not interested in facts. He wants my opinion.

What do you think is wrong with your nose? Is it your own idea, or has someone else influenced you? If so, who?

I am certainly not going to tell him about Fats Russell. *My nose is not straight,* I write. *There is this humongous bump on it. I came to this conclusion all by myself with the help of my mirror.*

The next batch of questions deals with the rest of me.

Do I have allergies, particularly to drugs?

Do I bruise easily?

Do I have high blood pressure? Heart disease?

Then the questions focus on my parents and on my family's health history. Kate helps me answer these questions.

"This doctor wants to know everything about everyone," I grumble. "It's none of his business."

"It is his business," Kate disagrees, "exactly."

I return the questionnaire to the nurse. Waiting, I have the oddest feeling that I am far away from myself, dreaming myself in a dream. Perhaps I have thought about this visit too many times and acted it out in my mind.

There are other people in the office, waiting, but the only one there with a really classy nose is Kate. Directly opposite from us sits a thin older woman in mourning clothes. Even her stockings are black. She has a small smashed nose like a fig, a hopeless nose. Why didn't she ever do anything about it? I wonder. Sitting next to her is a young woman, her daughter, I guess, with a so-so nose. Not nearly as bad as the mother's, but with flared nostrils — a trifle too wide.

I think it is nice that this sad-looking woman in mourning is taking the trouble — during her own trouble — to help her daughter get her nose corrected. Probably the mother doesn't want her child to suffer as she has suffered.

The daughter begins to whisper, loudly, to the mother, and it becomes so interesting I watch them over the top edge of my *Rolling Stone*. There is a major war going on.

"You look fine," the daughter repeats several times. "Fine. Perfect!"

"I've told you, Janet. I have always hated my nose."

"Daddy's not even dead a year."

"What's that got to do with my nose?"

"You're practically a senior citizen."

"I don't care. I want to do it."

"It costs so much."

The mother turns in her chair and glares. "It's my money, Janet. Daddy left it to *me*."

"But why bother about it now? Who's going to notice?"

"The undertaker. Since I'm almost dead and buried in your mind, the undertaker, at least, will get to admire my new profile."

Janet is so mad, she is speechless.

"So, do me a favor," the mother continues, "leave. You invited yourself along. I don't want you here. I don't need your consent."

Out storms Miss Huffy. I feel like jumping up and

▼

shouting, "Bravo!" The mother relaxes. She reaches for a magazine. Not *Better Homes* . . . but *Forbes*. Never judge by appearances, I tell myself. Janet's mother is a lot more than she seems.

Sitting over in the corner is a young man really dressed up in a three-piece gray suit. He doesn't have too bad a nose. It's a trifle long. It reaches down into his black mustache a little, but it sort of suits his face. Horn-rims. Black hair. He will look the same way with a shorter nose. A nerd. But he sits hunched forward, chin in hand, fingers cupping the nose as a shield, the way I often sit. I sympathize. If it hurts that much, get it fixed. Do it. DO IT! No one should have to sit like that.

The others are ahead of us. Dr. Ricci comes out to greet each client. A tall, thin older man with intense black eyes and a sexy smile, he wears a white work-coat much like the ones we wear at YIN/YANG/YUMMY. In white, on him, it looks classy.

Finally, it is my turn. He comes out, my questionnaire in his hand. "Good evening. I am Dr. Ricci." He is suave, confident, right out of *General Hospital*.

"I'm Kate Trevor." Kate offers her hand. "This is my sister, Annie, who is interested in a nose operation."

He doesn't even look at my nose. He simply shakes my hand and smiles at me, then leads the way into an inner office. "Sit down, ladies." He moves to sit behind the large, littered desk. We are in a spacious square room painted white, with sink, scale, cabinets filled with instruments, and shelves with bottles and

▼

boxes on them. On the walls hang pictures in pairs, Befores and Afters. Noses galore. Miracles. I am not exaggerating. The Afters are miracles.

To Kate, he says cordially, "So you're Charlie's fiancée. I am delighted to meet you. Charlie is one of the pivotal people in our hospital. Without him, we'd be back in the nineteenth century; our machines would all stop running. They'd grind to a halt, and we'd have to return to primitive instruments."

Pleasure makes Kate blush. Charlie had been an all-around fine athlete in high school, and then, afterward, nothing happened. He'd pumped gas, waited tables, done unrewarding jobs, until his love of machines led him to medical technology. Kate always knew he was smart, but no one in his family ever had the time to notice or encourage him, and his teachers hadn't helped, either. He, himself, had never been sure. Dr. Ricci's comments are a gift she will pass on to Charlie gladly.

"Annie or Ms. Trevor, which would you prefer I call you?"

"Annie. I'm used to it."

"Fine. You are in high school?"

I nod.

"Not fifteen yet?"

"In less than a month I will be."

"The best age for rhinoplasty."

I stare at him. "What?"

"Rhinoplasty. Rhino is Greek for nose. Plasty means formation." He smiles. "I will give you some literature to read while you are making up your mind. This is a very big step you are considering. You can't be ignorant. You must learn all you can about it."

I agree.

"You know you need parental consent?"

"Both parents?"

"One is enough, but if both approve, it's even better."

"I have to work on my father — if I decide to do it. To tell you the truth, Dr. Ricci, I don't think I could do it if he disapproved. Even if my mother signed."

The doctor nods. "Now let's talk about your nose." He looks over the questionnaire, noting what I have written. "All right. You tell me exactly how you feel about your nose."

"I hate it. It's ugly. It's got this bump — "

"Have you always felt this way about it?"

I hesitate. "I guess I didn't think about it much when I was very young."

"How much do you think about it now?"

"All the time."

"What do you think?"

"I wish it would disappear."

He just listens.

"I'd like to be pretty."

He doesn't make nice. He doesn't tell me I'm pretty. He just sits there, resting his hands on the desk. I look at his fingers, fairly ordinary-looking fingers. Somehow I expect a surgeon's hands to be something special. His are strong and clean-looking, but nothing remarkable. When you think how much people trust those fingers and hands to remake their faces! I don't know what I expected.

"I can probably make you a bit prettier," he says gravely, "but you must not have any illusions about this kind of operation. Your face now is your face afterward. Your personality is your personality. You will remain largely the same."

I understand why it's necessary for him to say all this; though it seems simple, he is actually correct that in my head I have created a better, more gifted, glamorous, and beautiful *After*-Annie. He is warning me that is not going to happen.

"What's the procedure, Doctor?" Kate asks.

"Through a remarkable machine — a video computer — I can actually project the redesign of Annie's face. It's done with imaging. I project an image of your face onto the computer monitor, and then I manipulate the image. I redraw it until we get the result we want.

"The computer image gives you a good idea of how you'll look. Understand, this video image can only be altered within the severe limits of the way your face is structured."

"Sounds amazing," Kate says.

"It is," the doctor agrees. "I will also show you a bunch of Before and After pictures so you can see what happened to patients with noses like yours. And, of course, we'll take some pictures of you from various angles and study them."

"Will we know before the operation what I'll look like?"

"We'll guess. But we won't know. The best rhino-

▼

113

plasty results in an absolutely natural appearance. If it's a really successful operation, your nose will look exactly right on your face. Like nothing happened."

"That's for me!"

"Not so fast. First, you have to go home and think about it. And read up a little on plastic surgery. It's an ancient art." He opens a desk drawer and selects a number of papers from folders. "If you decide you want to go for it, just call and make the preliminary appointment with my nurse."

"How long will the whole thing take?"

"I like to do the operation at Cloverdale Hospital. A day or so there, and you can go home. There will be swelling and discoloration at first, but that goes away pretty quickly. By ten days to two weeks, you are ready to face the world again with a streamlined nose."

The thought is pure ecstasy.

"The total cost will be four thousand dollars, and it is not covered by health insurance," Dr. Ricci reminds us. "We can arrange to have you pay it off slowly without additional charges. But it is still a lot of money."

"I know," I say.

"Give this careful thought, Annie. It's not a toss-the-coin decision."

We leave, me holding a handful of pamphlets.

"I like him," Kate says, outside. "I trust him. He's direct and he's honest."

I feel my nose. Maybe the bump has vanished? No such luck.

▼

"Now you have to do your homework," Kate says. "Read that stuff carefully. Whatever you decide, I'm with you."

"I'll read it all, but I think I've already decided. Now I only have to persuade Daddy and Grandpa and earn a lot of money."

"Nothing to it," she says lightly. "A piece of cake."

"More like a dog biscuit," I say. "Hard, hard, hard!"

At the end of this eventful day, I take out the letter with the Polaroid pictures for Grandpa that I've been carrying around, stamped, ready to mail. I have had my musical omen — and I know my own mind — so the last thing I do before bed is run out and mail it.

FOURTEEN

One pleasure Bob and I can afford because it's free
is going jogging on the cool, early spring nights after
we work our shifts at YIN/YANG/YUMMY or do our
homework. We stay away from Bob's town, Edison,
because there are gangs hanging around at the
Burger King, and on the street corners there are
pushers peddling crack and pot in the darkness. In
Cloverdale, my town, which is just a little distance
away — towns are linked in a chain close to each
other all through north Jersey — no stores are open
at night, and Bob and I have the dark silent streets
to ourselves. Cloverdale is quiet, and the night air
smells sweet. The bus stops have sheltered benches
and the buses don't run late, so the benches are always empty.

Joggers require occasional way stations to rest.

We run a mile or so. Then we sit and neck. Then we run some more. Then it is time to sit again. Bob is very careful to keep the necking under control. He's determined not to repeat the mistake his parents made; he doesn't want *to have to* get married. It's on his mind constantly, he says, almost as much as sex is. Almost.

Sometimes we sit together silently, dreaming, enjoying the gentle night. Particularly after a frantic day in YIN/YANG/YUMMY, with neurotic customers and stuck register drawers and torn tapes, with Mr. Buehler trying to do too much, the quiet darkness is a pleasure.

This is a special night, Bob's seventeenth birthday, and we get a later start than usual. Mr. Buehler, who long ago recognized that Bob had what he calls "an artistic eye," has Bob setting up a huge avocado-papaya-pineapple display. It is spectacular, but it takes an extra hour to complete. I am delighted to add another hour working at check-out while I wait for Bob to finish.

I am so incredibly glad I'm there when Ms. Campion, in a long flowered skirt and red tank top and huge spirally earrings, suddenly puts in an appearance. I happen to know she lives in Manhattan, so I doubt she is here for dandelion greens.

"I almost didn't know you in that outfit," she says to me. "Can you tell me where I can find Cal?"

For a minute, in the confusion, my mental register runs a blank tape.

▼

"Mr. Buehler — " she prompts.

"In that little office," I point, and she goes.

The next customer on my check-out line, a sturdy lady with a man's haircut, has a whole cartful of Ohsawa organic foods: soba and kuzu, shiso leaves, and soft plums. The works.

My eyes are on Ms. Campion. The customer shifts on her feet and begins to mutter about how slow I am, but I just *have* to watch my teacher.

"Sorry," I say, "the register is overheated, and I have to wait a minute to cool it. Otherwise, the tape starts to burn and sets off the smoke alarms. First thing you know, they have to evacuate the store."

The customer pulls a copy of *Macromuse* from the rack and begins to riffle through it. I watch Ms. Campion knock on the office door.

The door opens, and there is Mr. Buehler, smiling. Then he is grinning. Never have I seen such joy on his face. Especially not on busy days. Instead of coming out, he takes her hand and draws her inside and shuts the door. That office is about four feet wide. There is a chair, a desk, and bookshelves. There is no room to move around.

"Your register must be frozen by now," my customer observes. I guess *Macromuse* doesn't have articles that grab customers like the *National Enquirer* does at regular supermarket check-outs.

I go back to work happily. Whatever Mr. Buehler and Ms. Campion are doing, they have my best wishes. One day I might be their maid of honor. And I bet I could make up the menu for the wedding

▼

feast. I'm handling most of the ingredients right now as I begin to bag this enormous order, assuring the lady three different times that the bags are biodegradable.

When Bob and I finally finish work, we go to my house and get into our running clothes and drop off the cameras.

We jog a good distance and then we sit. "Happy birthday," I say, kissing him and then giving him the name-bracelet I've bought. We kiss and then we kiss some more and some more. "What a nice surprise party!" he murmurs. "You shouldn't have done it." He draws me closer. It's warm and exciting and wonderful. Our exercise clothes are all sweaty, smelly, in fact. We sit so close, we are breathing together like one human being. Suddenly, Bob pushes me away a little and slides toward the end of the bench. "Our kids will be born when *we* want them," he whispers fiercely.

"Our kids?" I lick my lips, which feel slightly bruised in a lovely way. "You haven't even asked me yet."

"I don't have to, do I, Annie?" He slides back toward me to take hold of my chin and move my face so he can look into my eyes. "Do I?"

I giggle and move right up close to him. "Sure you do."

"We're both too young. Especially you," he protests, then he slips down off the bench onto his knees. Clasping his hands dramatically before him like a goon, he implores, "Ms. Trevor, will you wait till I can claim your hand in marriage?"

My giggling gets out of control. When I can answer, I gasp, "Mistah Pritchitt, take my hand *right* now." I dangle it loosely before him.

He grabs my hand and kisses the palm and then swoops me into a gigantic hug. "I'll claim the rest in a few years. Listen, I'm on my way to fame and fortune. Mr. Buehler has upped my pay a dollar an hour."

"You're kidding."

"No. I talked him into it. He wants me to work only on food displays. You know I did the Thanksgiving cornucopias, and I helped the guy who came in to do the Christmas windows. He says maybe he'll let me do the entire Easter display instead of hiring a professional. If I'm still around — "

"Where are you going?"

"I don't know, Annie."

"Your father again?"

"Not again. Still. Forever. It never stops, only now it's getting worse. It's like he can't bear the idea that I'm going to have a high school diploma — and he doesn't have one. He keeps grumbling that I'm too big for my boots. My mother says it's that he can't stand having another man in the house with him. It's not anything I do. It's just that I'm there."

I stroke his hair. "Patience," I urge. "Once you're out of school, it will be easier. You can pay your own way or you can move out."

"I know. Look, let's not talk about it anymore.

▼

There's nothing I can do about him." He lapses into silence.

"Hey. It's your birthday. Don't spoil the party."

"Sorry. Tell me something interesting."

"Tonight I have not one, but two hot items." First I tell him about Ms. Campion in her red tank top and jazzy skirt coming into the store. That pleases him. Then I move on. "You are about to hear the newest international authority on rhinoplasty give her spellbinding spiel."

"Rhino-what?"

"Nose jobs. Sit still and listen. Rhino is Greek for nose. Plasty means formation."

"You been doing research or something?"

"Something. Kate and I went to see this sexy, older, plastic surgeon to talk about it. He gave me some pamphlets, and I've been reading them."

"You're really hooked on the subject, aren't you, kid?"

I nod. "I learned some fascinating stuff. How long do you think they've been doing nose jobs?"

"Mmm. I guess it's a fairly modern operation. A wild guess — as much as a hundred years?"

I laugh my superior laugh high in my throat. "Nose jobs date back to the sixth century B.C., maybe earlier."

"Really?"

"They have these records going all the way back. A famous ancient doctor, a Hindu in India named Susruta, wrote descriptions of how to reconstruct a nose. He told exactly how it was done."

▼

"Why were they doing that operation in those days? It must have been painful and dangerous. Was it to improve their looks?"

"A good question. The answer is in a way, yes, and in a way, no. Turns out this was an important operation in India and a bunch of other old countries because in those places the punishment for thievery and adultery was to cut off the nose of the offender.

" 'Along came a blackbird,' " I sing, " 'and snipped off his nose.' "

I demonstrate with my two bent fingers and his nose.

"But I'm innocent — " he protests.

"That's just a warning."

My information about the ancient world really interests him. "How many thieves and adulterers were there?" he wonders.

"Many, I guess, because it seems to have been a fairly common operation, common enough so they figured out this really neat system for rebuilding noses out of forehead skin. They still use the method today. It's called the Indian method of rhinoplasty."

Bob is both fascinated and repelled. "Did the pamphlets tell you how they did it?"

"Yes. They cut an inverted triangle in the forehead skin just above the nose, leaving a small strip attached between the eyes to preserve circulation. The skin is half-twisted around and a new nose is fashioned."

"It's brilliant."

▼

I agree. "These days the nose job is a quick and easy operation. Dr. Ricci figures overnight in the hospital, and then ten days or so for recovery. After that, a new Annie Trevor will appear, a little battered-looking at first, but definitely a new Annie Trevor. No more 'Bump.' "

"I like the old Annie."

"Won't you want the hand of the new one?"

"I guess the hand will stay the same."

"Bob, I want this operation. I have to have this operation."

"How much will it cost?"

"Four thousand dollars."

"It better be a new Annie Trevor! How will you ever pay for it?"

"The doctor says I can pay it off slowly — no interest."

Bob begins to laugh. "If you don't pay, that's thievery. You've stolen his services. Does he get to take your nose back?"

"Very funny." I elbow him in the ribs. "Stop laughing at me."

He stops. "I don't know why, Annie, but there is something particularly funny about noses."

"Think I should go for it?"

"It's your nose."

"You wouldn't know that from the way my father and grandfather act."

"Give them a little time. They'll get used to the idea. You're very persuasive. You've persuaded me."

"Have I? That's wonderful."

▼

"You've persuaded me that you need the operation. For your own peculiar reasons. You haven't persuaded me that you've got an ugly nose." He kisses the tip of it. "I'll miss it," he says.

He is sweet.

FIFTEEN

Bob and I were both born — he in March and I in April — under the sign of Aries, the ram, named for the Golden Fleece in mythology, the first sign of the zodiac. All that astrology stuff used to be important to me. In grade school, I looked up my horoscope every night in the newspaper to prepare myself for the next day. Then, in my general science class, my teacher told us astrology was a pseudo-science and she said it was inexact. That really shook me up. She argued that the astral calculations were done by the Babylonians maybe two thousand years ago before there were accurate instruments to tell what was truly going on in the skies. "Do you really believe," she asked us, "that what happens to you is governed by stars and planets whose paths are mistakenly plotted?"

No. I honestly do not believe that. I swear it. But

▼

it is tempting. Because, for whatever reason, some months are worse than other months. March turns out to be the worst month of my entire life. Bob's, too. A disaster. If I could wipe out one period of my life — just remove it so that time never happened — I would erase March forever.

First of all, I never even get a chance at persuading Grandpa about my operation. He gets sick too fast. In fact, he nearly dies with his hammer in his hand. Rather, a screwdriver. The whole thing is crazy; he is putting the finishing touches, brass handles, on an oak liquor cabinet at eleven at night while the customer waits — a rush job because the guy needs his cabinet for a housewarming party the next day — when suddenly Grandpa begins gasping for air and crumpling over from wrenching pains. His customer frantically phones the police, then carries Grandpa over to his Murphy bed.

We don't know anything about it until that part is all over, until the police and the medics have taken him off to the Intensive Care Unit at Cloverdale Hospital. Soon as I hear about it, I know just what brought it on. Stress. My letter and those awful Polaroid shots. I know who is responsible for this attack. Me. I am frantic with guilt. How could I burden a sick old man who had said he didn't want to hear about it? How could I?

We all go to the hospital as soon as we can. Grandpa is critically ill, but resting comfortably when we get there. So the nurse says. He looks uncomfortable to me, lying under plastic (How he hates plastic!) like some display, assisted by various tubes

▼

and dripping bottles and machines that only Charlie among us understands.

"They're helping him breathe," Charlie explains to me. "His lungs have lost their elasticity, so he can't take in enough oxygen. But he's going to be fine." He squeezes my hand. "Honest, kid, he really is."

Of course my letter didn't cause the condition, but it must have upset him a lot. Those pictures that I made Bob take are so ugly. If only I had not been so selfish!

Emphysema seems to shrink a person. Grandpa looks smaller and very frail in the plastic tent. He is the color of old paper, his eyes agates in the pallor. His eyes stay open, watching us, and it seems to me his mouth twitches in a kind of weak smile. The nurse urges us to make it a very short visit. "Don't try to talk to him," she warns. "He's very tired and needs rest."

We take her advice. The others each go by the foot of his bed and wish him good-night, but I blow him a kiss, and — is it possible? I think I see his eyes twinkle.

He's got to be all right. I will it! He's got to be, just so we can make up, be friends again. I couldn't bear it if he died, especially if he died angry with me because we'd argued and he thought I was vain and obsessed. We had been best of friends my whole lifetime. We had spent the Sundays of my childhood feeding the ducks at the Bronx Zoo. Grandpa, I pray silently, get better so I can tell you how sorry I am that we argued about the Trevor nose. It's not as important as our being friends. Nothing is. Nothing.

▼

I'll even live with my nose the way it is and never mention it again, I promise, if you get well. I offer this sacrifice to God.

My father is so sad, I want to comfort him, but, instead, when I try to, I blurt out my own guilty part in all of this. "I never should have sent him the letter," I say regretfully. "I never should have unloaded my troubles on him."

Daddy manages a tired smile. "Annie, you really are a nice kid. Your letter didn't do this. Grandpa's smoking for fifty years did it. He knows that. We all know it."

"But I upset him insulting the family nose like that."

Daddy ruffles my hair. "Don't worry about it. We Trevors are tough." He looks at me speculatively. "The nose really bothers you that much?"

I nod.

"We'll talk about it when Grandpa gets better."

I kiss him. It's a victory of sorts, though it comes too late to have much meaning.

Any emphysema attack is serious, nothing a person, particularly an elderly person, recovers from fast. It takes weeks. First, they have to get Grandpa off continuous oxygen. He spits a great deal. It's very important that his respiratory passages are kept clear. With emphysema, that's hard to do. His strength must be built up.

As soon as he can talk, he makes a vow. "As God is my witness, I will never smoke again!" He means it this time, we can tell. Then, reading everyone's mind, he says, "I know. Better late then never." He blames only himself for his weakness. "You don't have to say it."

One thing in Grandpa's favor is his love of life. Daddy reminds us of this many times during the long illness to reassure himself and the rest of us. "My father doesn't give up. He understands that life is to be lived fully to the very last moment."

Slowly, as Grandpa gains strength, I can see Daddy dreading what must come next. A struggle. When Grandpa is well enough to be discharged from the hospital, he will not be well enough to live at home alone. Days he is okay because people come by constantly, neighbors look in, and he has his old buddies. But nights are too dangerous. My parents make up their minds; he will come and stay in our house. Kate and I will manage in the living room, and Grandpa can have our room. (How wise Charlie was not to take my advice and marry Kate and move in with us. Where would they go now? Charlie is nice enough not to mention this.)

We all know that before Grandpa can be convinced to move in, there will be a fierce battle.

"I'll get the doctor to forbid him to live alone," Daddy resolves. "If that guy had not been there late at night to pick up his cabinet, there's no question but Grandpa would have died. We can't take a chance like that again." But neither can Daddy chance an argument with Grandpa in his weak condition. To even so much as hint that he might have to live away from his tools and workshop and wood is to look for a fight. And to tell him he has to move in with us — though he loves us — would be to deliver a knock-out blow. Grandpa has a lifelong sense of independence.

Ah, but Grandpa is smart, smarter than the rest of us. He lies there convalescing and being outrageously cranky, even for him. "They roll me around and poke me and stick me," he gripes. "Vicious people dressed all in white so they'll look merciful and oh so saintly. Sadists, that's who goes into medicine nowadays. They ought to all be wearing red. Scarlet!"

Whenever a nurse comes to help him change his bedgown, he really takes off. "What kind of person gives a man a dress to wear in bed? It doesn't cover me, it creeps up on me until it nearly strangles me like a noose. How many patients do you lose a year garroted by these bedgowns?" I think he hates the hospital garments even worse than he hates plastic.

And all the while he is lying there complaining and recovering, he is plotting, making plans, formulating his own private complicated visions. One characteristic of Grandpa's has always impressed me: how he can keep things to himself. My secrets were always safe with him, and he keeps his own secrets as well. He has the greatest contempt for idle gossip. He says gossip is murder, murder of someone's reputation, and that is one crime he is not going to be guilty of. And he isn't; he doesn't talk about people behind their backs or put them down. He lets them be. Oh, he'll criticize some stupid act when he hears of it, but, if possible, to the one who committed it. The perpetrator. Grandpa likes that word.

So we watch him seemingly engrossed in the details of his own convalescence: taking in fluids; doing various light exercises and then increasing the exercises in number and difficulty as he grows stronger; monitoring the drugs he is getting and ascertaining what each one is for, always checking to be sure he is getting the correct dosage and getting it on time. When he catches the hospital staff in the slightest error — white toast instead of wheat/where is his prune juice?/they didn't make the bed with fresh linen — he really crows. Grandpa is more than a bit of a pest as a patient, for he hates hospitals. He wants out as soon as possible.

No one has any idea, as he gripes and gains strength, of what the world's worst patient is thinking.

SIXTEEN

I am nearly zapped by this month of March. I come to understand that there are no boundaries to the pain felt by people who love each other. When someone you love is suffering, you suffer with him. Grandpa's sickness is frightening; it makes me feel guilty and depressed on these cold, bleak, windy days.

One afternoon I am cheered up by Dee's news. She has ordered her precious contacts, without phony color. "Another two weeks and I can pick them up and pay for them," she confides to me happily. "No more four-eyes ever again." I hug her for joy.

Immediately afterward, Bob is struck by disaster.

Monday afternoon he is waiting for me outside school after three, standing at the bike rack, looking the way he looked that awful night in the cold-storage room at YIN/YANG/YUMMY. As if the world had fallen in.

▼

"My father got the cameras, Annie."

I didn't think I heard right.

You have to know how much Bob loves those cameras, how he worked nights and twelve-hour-day shifts during the summer vacations to get them, how he cares for them, handling them with tenderness and protecting them from the bad weather and from getting knocked around. I like to kid him. "If there were a fire and you had to save either me or your cameras, which would you save?"

"No contest," he says. "You are much more easily replaceable — and less expensive." Then he ducks automatically, anticipating the tickling attack.

Those cameras are his bionic extra limbs grafted on; they are his sensors, and he depends on them and will be crippled without them.

"Why? Why did he take them?" I ask. "He must be hiding them to tease you. He'll give them back."

Bob shakes his head. His throat is so choked up, he can barely speak. "He sold them."

"Did he lose his job? Does he need money that bad? I thought construction work was such a hot deal."

"He did it to teach me a lesson."

"What lesson?"

"That picture-taking is not man's work."

"But they are *your* cameras. *You* paid for them."

"What does that matter? They were in *his* house."

Sometimes there is nothing more to be said, and the only decent, honest thing to do is to shut up. Otherwise, the words are all false, and both the speaker and the hearer know it. Bob's father is a bully. A drunken bully. There isn't any new thing in this world I can come up with to say about living with a drunken bully.

There *is* one new thing I can say: *Run away! Run for your life!* But I don't want to say it.

"How did he get them, Bob?"

"Easy. You know I stayed for a double-shift with Mr. Buehler yesterday. Remember the kind of day it was?"

"Sure. Everyone in the county came in looking for his granola and Tummy Mint tea. First day we ever ran out of Evian Natural Spring Water. People were buying like the drought was at hand."

"Right. I was so tired when I got home, I just fell asleep in my clothes. I never even got into bed, just flopped down on the cover with my cameras. And I guess I was so dead asleep I didn't hear him come in or feel him take them."

"Maybe your mother put them away for you. How do you know he took them? How do you know he sold them?"

"Because I asked her as soon as I woke up this morning and saw they were missing. Then I went out to the job he's working on."

"I knew you missed school. I looked for you. Did you find him?"

"I found him all right. Sitting on a low girder, drinking a beer. He wasn't overjoyed to see me. 'What you doin' here, boy?' he asked me. 'How come you're not wastin' more time in that crazy school?'

" 'My cameras are missing.'

▼

" 'Eh? That so?' He was laughing at me, really enjoying it.

" 'Where are they?' I asked him. 'What did you do with them?'

" 'They're gone, boy.' He leaned his head way back and chugged the rest of the beer. Then he belched.

" 'What do you mean *gone*?' I asked, though I think I already knew.

" 'Gone means gone. Plain English. I sold 'em to a buddy of mine who's got a new kid he wants to take pictures of.'

" 'They were my cameras. I earned the money for them.'

"He got up and moved real close to me so he was talking in my face practically. 'Now you listen to me. I've been feedin' you and clothin' you too long. I don' wanna hear nothin' about cameras no more. Unnerstan'? Nothin'. Now you get the hell outta here. I'm a workin' man. I don' sit aroun' readin' picture books.'

"I felt like killing him," Bob said dully. "If I'd had a gun — or a knife — "

I have never seen him so shaken up. His face is coated with a film of sweat, and his body is trembling.

"Don't talk like that. You couldn't hurt anyone, even him. You know it."

"I've always thought that. I prided myself in knowing that. But this morning if I could have hurt him, I would have, I swear."

"What will you do now?"

▼

"I don't know. My mother says let it pass. Now that the cameras are gone, maybe he'll let up on me. He hated them so. She just wants to see me graduate, the first of her kin ever to do it. I'd like that for her sake — and for my sake. If not for that, I'd get out today, tonight, before he comes home. I don't want to do that to her. She's had nothing but disappointments in her life — nothing."

"Bob, you'd better go talk to Dean Packard."

"What good would that do?"

"It can't hurt. He might have some ideas."

"I don't need ideas. I need a miracle."

"He comes from a religious family."

That got a feeble try at a smile.

"Do it for me," I ask. "Because I'm so scared for you, and I can't think of any way to help you. Please," I plead. "Please."

"All right. Tomorrow morning, before Home-room."

"Let's go running," I propose. "Let's get into our sweats and forget about everything else except going the distance."

And that's what we do, silently. We go the entire length — from one end of Cloverdale to the other — together, but separately in our heads — till we are winded and weary. We don't take any rests at the bus stop shelters. We just run.

And the running helps.

Bob keeps his word. He goes right in to see Dean Packard, who is glad to see him, sorry to hear about the cameras, but really gratified that Bob had enough

▼

trust and confidence in him not to just take off —
but to come to him with his troubles.

"Not that there's so much I can do for you," the
dean confesses, "besides sympathize. And you already knew that.

"I think your mother is probably right. Things
should ease up now that he's gotten rid of the cameras and showed you who's boss. So, if you can hang
in there for another couple of months — after all
you've managed it for seventeen years — and get
your diploma, you can move on."

"Thanks," Bob says. "I didn't expect you to do
anything for me. I just wanted you to know in
case — " He makes a move to go.

"No," says the dean, stopping him short, "don't let
him make you do things you'll be sorry for. I'm talking about violence. If it gets out of control, run. Don't
just walk. *Run!* I'll give you my home phone number,
so you can always reach me here or at home." He
scrawls the numbers on a memo slip. "One thing
more. You should think about the military. I'm no
recruiter — but it's one answer for someone with
intelligence and skills like your camera work. There
might be a chance for you to learn more about things
that interest you, and what you already know could
be of use. I'll make some phone calls and see what
I can come up with for a man of your background.
Okay?"

Of course it's okay. Bob is not crazy to enlist, but
he's thought of it many times as a possible way out —
a lifeline.

No high school faculty member had ever called

▼

him a "man" before. Not even Ms. Campion, who thinks he's talented; she sees him as a talented kid. Mostly the teachers are Mr. Raymond halved; they enjoy cutting him down.

Dean Packard calling him a man gives him a sense of dignity on the morning when he most needs it.

He leaves the dean's office determined to tiptoe even more cautiously around his father — for just a little longer. If he takes real care and watches what he does, if he just stays out of Pritchitt Senior's way, he will make it.

It's a demeaning and dangerous game, one he despises, but the stakes are high, and he has no option. He is in it for his life.

SEVENTEEN

April first is my birthday. It's no easy thing to be born on April Fool's Day. Nobody passes up the chance to admire Mother Nature's judgment. . . . It's weird how many people think the same jokes are so original. "Your parents sure got a trick played on them. You!"

Even if Grandpa were not sick, I wouldn't have had a big birthday party. My family doesn't go in for parties. Money is scarce, and they have this thing about buying on credit, and, we're kind of private. We would have had a small celebration at home. With Grandpa recuperating in the hospital, we take the party to him.

Mom bakes me a sour-cream chocolate layer cake; we all get dressed up, me in a really good-looking denim skirt and jacket I choose (Mom still has trouble with denim for dresswear, but she pays for it).

▼

Grandpa is sitting up in bed, propped upright by three fat pillows and the mechanically slanted upper half of his bed. His white hair has been carefully combed, he is shaved, and his mustache is brushed. And he is not wearing the hated hospital bedgown! He is wearing eye-boggling bright-red flannel pajamas, a gift from my parents. He looks elegant. His favorite nurse, Mrs. Robins, has prepared him.

Bob wears a shirt, tie, and navy blazer for the occasion. He looks elegant, too. And handsome. (Vickie Upham's crimson claws would turn green with envy if she saw him.)

We joke around a lot. I blow out my fifteen-plus-one-for-good-luck pink candles after I make my wish, which remains secret. It concerns one other person, and, perhaps, a ring in the future.

Mom and Dad give me a gift certificate to The Gap because Mom says, "I know any clothes I buy for you will not be *plej fenomenega!*" (I've got to get her a book on Esperanto. It's *her* language.) Kate and Charlie give me a Walkman. Bob gives me Nirvana and U2 cassettes.

What a cake! Thick, smooth, luscious chocolate. My mother makes the supreme chocolate cake.

When we finish eating (Bob and I have two slices apiece because we're growing children), and we've gathered up all the paper plates and plastic forks and other junk, Grandpa says, "Listen, everybody, I didn't give Annie my gift yet. I meant to make her a music unit to hold her records and cassettes, but my lungs interfered. I have something to say to all of

▼

you, so settle down and hear me out. Annie, listen carefully."

Whatever plan he's been sitting on silently is to be hatched now.

So Mom and Dad sit on the two visitors' chairs, and the rest of us group around the foot of the bed.

"I've had a lot of time here to think," Grandpa begins, "about my life and some dumb things I did, like starting to smoke" — he says grimly " — and some smart things I did, like marrying young. I've made some important decisions for this family. I'm still head of the Trevor family and perfectly capable of making decisions." He peers at Daddy defiantly. "I'm not asking. I'm telling.

"I know what you're about to spring on me. I wasn't born yesterday. I am *not* going to any nursing home or any senior citizens residence. I will not live under anyone else's roof. I am not going to be a burden."

"You could never be a burden," Mom says.

He smiles. He knows she means it: Mrs. Soft-heart Trevor.

"But you can be a stubborn nuisance," Daddy assures him.

Grandpa acknowledges that with a dip of his head. "I've got my own agenda. I'm the oldest one here, and with age comes either senility or wisdom. I've examined my own head carefully and decided I'm not senile. So I must be wise. I figure if God spared me this long, He did it for some purpose. So — "

I see Daddy sit up straighter, bracing himself for

▼

some cockamamie proposal that will be impossible.

"You all know that I made my will a while ago, so it's no secret that when I die, all my worldly goods will go to my son to use as he sees fit. Well, I've decided to alter that arrangement. I want a hand in distributing my bit of property now, while I'm still able to supervise and enjoy it."

Grandpa pauses to sip some Bourassa Canadian Glacial Water. Mr. Buehler, when he heard that Grandpa was hospitalized with emphysema, sent over a case of the stuff for him. (Mr. Buehler is blooming these days, and it's not on brown rice.)

"Now call Mrs. Robins, the nurse. She helped me by doing the writing for me." Grandpa closes his eyes and relaxes on the pillow, while Charlie goes looking for the nurse.

In she comes, a pretty young woman, a co-conspirator by the gleeful look on her face.

"Nurse, will you read my family our document?" Grandpa asks.

"*Your* document, Mr. Trevor. I only did the writing."

I don't blame her for disclaiming responsibility for whatever is coming. Grandpa's mind goes its own way.

"Go on and read."

She reaches into the drawer of the white metal night table and takes out an envelope. " 'I, William Trevor, being of sound mind, do make the following disposition of my property to take effect as of this date and to supersede all previous wills.

" 'To my granddaughter, Kate Trevor, and her fi-

▼

ancé, Charlie Thompson, I sell my house, 111 Grove Street, Cloverdale, New Jersey, with all its furnishings, for whatever down payment they can manage immediately, total cost and subsequent payments to be worked out. I do this on condition that they occupy the house as soon as they are married, and on the further condition that they allow me to remain as their tenant in the basement for as long as I live. Upon my death, the house is theirs free and clear.' "

"Grandpa," Kate whispers, "how incredible of you."

"I couldn't, sir," Charlie says. "I couldn't." He is suddenly very pale.

"Sure you can. You must. You'll be helping me out because I've nowhere to go from here if that house stays empty. Besides, Charlie, you're the only one in this crowd with skilled hands. You'll appreciate the tools. And you two should marry young. That's the best time. Nurse, go on."

" 'Until Kate and Charlie are married, I shall occupy the house and be cared for by a practical nurse to be paid for from my savings account.

" 'To my other granddaughter, Annie Trevor, whose fifteenth birthday we are celebrating today, I give three thousand dollars from my savings account to be added to her own money to meet the cost of a plastic surgery operation.' "

I cover my face with my hands, this time not to hide my nose but to hide my tears.

"Annie?" Grandpa says.

"You were so against it — "

"In principle I'm still against it." He rubs his nose.

"It's a good and honorable nose. But you write a strong letter, girl. Your boyfriend, on the other hand, takes terrible pictures. Son" — he looks sharply at Bob — "find another hobby. Those were the worst pictures I have ever seen."

Bob actually blushes. "I usually do better."

"I should hope so. I figured these were done to make Annie's point."

"My fault, Grandpa. He didn't want to take them."

He waves my explanations away. He had already figured things out. "What happened, Annie, is I had time here to realize that I don't understand a lot of what is going on today. It's all too fast. But I do understand something that grabs you and you can't shake free of it and it drives you crazy and whittles you down and won't let go. With me it was the smoking, and with you it's this nose business. So I decided if this operation will make you happy and make your life better, then you should have it. You'd get the money anyway when I died. This way I'll be around to see my happy grandchildren. I get *my* reward here and now." He looks over at Daddy. "Well, son. What do you think? I'm taking a kind of strong hand here with your family. Do you mind?"

"All my life you've surprised me," Daddy says quietly. "Why should you stop now?" He reaches over to take Grandpa's hand.

"Nurse Robins," Grandpa says, "show these folks out, please. I'm really tired. I'm going to sleep tonight without pills."

Outside his door, she says to us, "He's a remarkable man. He drives us all crazy here, but he's one of a kind."

"Thank you for everything," Daddy says. "We know that about him, but it bears saying. Sometimes we take it for granted."

EIGHTEEN

Two major Edison High School beautification projects are scheduled for the Easter recess, and neither one needs the approval of the school board. Dee is getting her contact lenses, and I am having the major face renovation. Kate and Charlie will be married in May, and I am determined to be the beautiful bridesmaid. People on either side of the aisle will gape in amazement when they see Annie Perfect Profile. *She could have been an Egyptian princess*, they'll think.

I contact Dr. Ricci's office, and they send the consent slip for my parents to sign. I can't wait!

That slip is really awesome. (Do I have to tell you what my mother said when she saw it?) "AUTHORIZATION FOR RHINOPLASTY" is the title, and then there is a single-spaced whole page of conditions we are agreeing to. In the old days in India, I'll bet the patients didn't have to sign anything: If someone

▼

came along without a nose, the doctor just went right to it. "Sit down on the rug," he'd say, "and close your eyes." Snip, snip, snip, and it was done.

First, we hereby authorize Dr. Ricci to change the shape of my nose; then, we agree that there are risks, complications, and alternative means of treatment, and Dr. Ricci has our consent to do whatever he thinks necessary; we authorize the use of anesthetics professionally administered; we understand that the results are not guaranteed, and that surgery is not an exact science; we understand that the two sides of the body are not the same and can never be made identical; we authorize the presence of observers in the operating room for the purpose of promoting medical education; finally, we will allow the taking of necessary clinical pictures, which Dr. Ricci will keep.

None of this bothers me much except the bit about the two sides of the human body not being the same. I was hoping for a perfect nose, pretty on both right and left profile. What if . . . ? I can't allow myself to dwell on dreadful what-ifs.

Daddy and Mom read it several times. Daddy consults with Grandpa about it; then Daddy signs and Mom signs as witness. It is a rather solemn ceremony. We send it back to Dr. Ricci with Charlie.

I begin to psych myself up as the first days of April pass. Patience is hard to come by. I have never wanted anything more. Dee, meanwhile, has been going to the ophthalmologist's office and trying the lenses on there and practicing with them. She can take them home anytime and pay the balance afterwards, but she won't do that. Her mother is opposed to her having the lenses. She wants her to concentrate on intellectual things — "higher things." So Dee is being very careful to conduct the whole deal very responsibly.

Grandpa is discharged from the hospital. The first thing he does when he gets back home is throw away his pipes, all of them, even the beloved meerschaum, and all the paraphernalia that goes with them: pouches, ashtrays, scrapers, pipe cleaners. He gets Daddy to post a sign on his front door, "NO SMOKING INSIDE. Reformed Smoker Now a Fanatic Within!" That's to protect himself from his buddies, several of whom are chain-smokers. He is feeling pretty good. A male practical nurse comes in the early evenings and spends his nights there. First time I ever met a male nurse; he is six feet three and two hundred pounds, but gentle. Grandpa seems to be coming along fine, and he keeps careful track of the progress of his two schemes: Kate and Charlie's wedding, and my nose job.

All the signs point to a really happy spring.

Briefly.

Then Bob disappears. For three days he is absent from school, and he doesn't phone or show up in the evenings and I can't reach him.

Finally, finally, about nine-thirty at night, when my imagination has me screaming silently, he phones.

"Bob, where've you been? I thought something happened to you."

▼

"Something did. Sorry. I couldn't help it. Can you come out for a walk?"

"Sure." I understand he can't talk freely. He must be calling from home.

"Pick you up in fifteen minutes."

I am washed, combed, made-up, perfumed — the works — long before he rings our doorbell.

"Mmm. You smell good," he greets me.

"Never mind that. Where have you been?"

"You won't believe me."

"I'll believe, I'll believe."

"I've been sleeping at Dean Packard's house in a room with seven-year-old identical twins. You wouldn't believe these kids, they're so mischievous."

I stop walking. "Will you please tell me what you are talking about? What were you doing in Dean Packard's house?"

"I had to get out of my father's house in the middle of the night. It was either YIN/YANG/YUMMY or Dean Packard's."

"Your father threw you out?"

"No." Bob's face was grim. "He came home drunk and he began to slap my mother around. He usually leaves her alone and concentrates on me. But this time — anyway, I tried to stop him. Lucky the neighbors called the cops, or we might have killed one another. Probably he would have killed me. I should have learned how to fight — to protect myself. My mother told me to go. She knew if I stayed there any longer, there'd be serious trouble."

"But how could you leave her?"

"She wouldn't come. I tried to talk her into leaving. We could make it, she and I. I can work. She won't leave him, she just won't. She says a marriage is a marriage, and he's not as bad as some." He laughs bitterly. "She thinks she'll be able to manage him once I'm not around. Usually, that's true. I'm the one he's always mad at."

"Bob, I'm so sorry. So very sorry."

"Me, too," he says wistfully. "You know what he keeps running on about now when he's drunk? No more cameras. Now what bugs him is Dean Packard. It's killing my father that there is an educated black man in a shirt and tie in a school office. That Pritchitt Senior was summoned by a black man.

"My father's wild. When I saw him going for my mother like that, I went berserk. So the best thing for me to do is stay away. Permanently."

"I'm so sorry," I repeat, because I haven't anything else to say. "Is Dean Packard in danger? Will your father come after you there? Will your father come after him?"

"My father is a coward. But I didn't tell you the good news."

"What good news?"

"I enlisted. In the Air Force, today. The dean got me a certified letter saying I had completed my high school work. I have, you know. The next few weeks are mostly seniors fooling around because the colleges have all made their decisions — anyway, I took it to the recruiting office in Hackensack and signed up." He puts his arms around me. "Will you miss me?"

▼

150

"More than you can believe." I hug him back. "The Air Force! Where will they send you?"

"First to Lackland Air Force Base, in San Antonio, Texas, for six weeks' basic training. After that, I don't know."

"How long is it for, Bob? Your enlistment?" I don't really want to hear the answer.

He looks straight at me. "Four years."

I am demolished. "Four years!"

He hugs me tighter. "I know it's a long time. But there are a lot of benefits, Annie. They run a community college in the Air Force where I can work for a two-year associate degree. They'll pay up to seventy-five percent of the tuition."

I'm crying. I just can't help it. Four years! "And what if there's a war?"

"I can't think about that. I've got to go, Annie. And I've got to trust our government not to get me killed meaninglessly."

I just stand there on the sidewalk, weeping. So much for the promises of spring and all my great plans and hopes.

"Stop crying," he says. "After the six hard weeks of basic training, I'll get a leave."

"Will you come back here?"

"Of course. Want to hear something funny? When I went back home tonight and told them what I'd done, my father was real proud of me. Enlisting is the first thing I ever did in my life that he approves of. You should have heard him. 'Come home any time, son, and give us a look at you in that uniform.' He's Mr. America now." Bob shakes his head rapidly to get rid of the demons. He says to me gently, "Anyway, I have to come back to see the new schnozz." He runs his forefinger lightly over the nose. "I'm sort of used to this one." He kisses the bump.

"You won't know me, soldier."

"I hope I will."

"Will I know you, Bob? After all, I'll still be just this little high school kid."

He laughs at me. "While I'll probably be a knockout in uniform, underneath I'll be me."

My throat is clogged. Too many feelings keep me from speaking.

"Annie, we're both so young, I know people will say it's stupid for us to make any promises. But I'd like to — if you would."

"Just let anyone say it's stupid to me, and I'll trample them."

He laughs and takes my hand. "I have my senior class ring. It's the cheaper kind, without the stone. Sorry about that. But I'd like you to have it. It's too big for you to wear except maybe on your thumb — "

"I'll wear it on a chain around my neck. It's so beautiful." Who says wishes don't come true? It isn't the ring I wished for. Still, it's really stunning, and it's a preliminary ring.

We find it necessary to conduct the ring ceremony formally by stopping at a bus shelter and kissing.

"I'm sorry I don't have anything to give you, Bob."

"Give me your promise you'll wait."

"I'll wait. What else would I do?"

Another kiss seals that promise. I am going to miss

▼

him terribly, as a boyfriend and even more as my best friend. "If they catch you reading on duty, they'll court-martial you," I tease. "No more petty Mr. Raymond's punishments."

"I'll be careful."

"I'll write to you a lot," I promise.

"And I'll write to you, Annie." He puts his arm around my waist, and I put mine around his, and we turn to walk back home. The moonlight gleams on the silent streets, silvering the whole town with glory. A kindly magical light, it seems.

"Funny," Bob says, "I don't feel trapped any more. Scared, yes. But doing this — getting away — changed the way I see myself and my life. It's not what I wanted, and I know it will be tough, but I can cope. With you back here waiting for me, I can cope with anything. The Air Force has already started its work making a man out of me. Not in my father's terms. In my own."

NINETEEN

Dr. Ricci does not believe in surprises. He wants his patients to be very well-informed during the entire course of treatment. I go back to his office several times for preliminary examinations and for orientation before my operation.

On one of my trips there, who should I see but Janet's mother, the woman in mourning clothes who I saw on my first visit, the one with the nose like a squashed fig, whose daughter minded that she wanted the operation. Janet's mother is a beauty now! She has a small, delicate nose in proportion to her face. No more shapeless mourning clothes. She is wearing a black suede suit. Fitted! What a transformation!

"You look beautiful," I say to her.

She is pleased. "So will you," she smiles.

Dr. Ricci projects my face onto the video computer

▼

screen and slowly and carefully through imaging he redesigns my nose. He is limited by what my facial structure will allow. The final picture he comes up with brings ecstasy to my heart. "Yes!" I say much too loudly. "Yes, yes, yes! Let's do it!"

He enjoys my excitement.

Dr. Ricci has prepared a little lecture on a video cassette. There he is, sitting at his desk, casual and charming, talking about the operation. I watch it over and over on the VCR in the tiny viewing room in his office, until I understand exactly what is going to happen to me. I absorb all the information, cramming the way I have learned from Dee to prepare for major tests. I really have it memorized.

This is the way it is done, he explains on tape.

The anesthesia is heavy sedation and local infiltration. A packing in the nose numbs the nose lining. Probably no pain is felt during the operation, and there is only a headache and a feeling of stuffiness afterward. Like a rotten head cold.

Since the operation is done through the nostrils, there won't be any scars. The surgery takes about two hours, and then a pressure dressing goes on the eyes to minimize swelling and bruises. The eye bandages come off the first morning after the operation. After the operation, a light packing goes inside the nose. It is taken out in a day or two. Also, after the operation, a splint is fixed outside the nose to hold it in proper position. The doctor takes the splint off on the fifth or sixth day.

Around the eyes you get swelling and bruising. The bruising usually disappears in a week, as does most

▼

of the swelling. Ice-cold compresses applied frequently hurry the healing along.

Because of the structure of the nose, it can only swell upward. During the first three weeks, this causes peculiar distortions of the face. It looks as if the nose was shortened too much. Don't worry. Once the swelling subsides and the nose comes down, the face will assume a more natural appearance. The tip of the nose may be unusually firm as the result of this operation. This gradually vanishes.

Healing time varies according to patients.

Don't bump your nose or exercise excessively during the first three weeks after surgery because these things prolong swelling and may cause bleeding. In general, take it easy.

Stay away from heat, hair dryers, hot water.

Easter vacation comes. For school kids, it means no school; for most people, it means spring: The earth will be green again. For religious people, it means renewed faith and hope. For me, it means surgery and then all the rest of those other meanings, but only after two weeks spent in hiding.

Mr. Buehler is cool about my not being able to work during the holidays. "It's a busy time," he says, "but I suppose your nose is a priority. I rather like your nose. It shows character. It is a bit irregular, but it's *your* nose, so you make the decision. Come back when you're healed — and let me know how you're doing."

Mr. Buehler is a nice guy ordinarily, but he is really fond of me since I brought him to our Living class.

▼

Ms. Campion has not been back to the store since that first visit, but from the way he looks these days and a certain rather laid-back quality to his behavior, I think the romance is moving along. I would love to know..

Mom checks me into the hospital and stays around waiting till the operation is over. I am to stay overnight, so she can come back early the next morning and take me home. I am ready, all psyched up for it, and my body is ready as well, for I've had nothing to eat for six hours before the operation.

Dr. Ricci is kind and very efficient. He talks to me a lot, trying to relax me while they are getting things ready. I won't go into gory details. It's not terrible, but it's no fun, either. What's important is, it gets done. It's over.

All through the miserable hours and days and weeks of convalescence that follow, Mom stays with me. She is tireless in her care of me. I haven't been really sick since I was a kid, so it's a trip back in time for her to be making special dishes: rice pudding stuffed with raisins and nuts, my favorite; and spareribs and lemon meringue pie. She reads to me when I am feeling down. We are reading *Pride and Prejudice*, by Jane Austen, about a mother trying to marry off her daughters, and it's fun. The mother is a panic.

"I'm glad you did it," Mom says to me, even before the bandages are off and we know what I look like. "I wouldn't have had the courage at your age — probably not even now — and I never would have spent the money because I didn't think my appearance was so important. Maybe it's my generation, I don't know."

I tell her about Janet's mother wearing widow's black and then later on. She is tremendously impressed.

"I don't know how that woman talked herself into doing it," she marvels, "if she was raised like me to believe you just accept your lot."

Mr. Buehler sends one of the security guards with a half-dozen plantains, a tin of cayenne pepper, and a message written on the back of a YIN/YANG/ YUMMY flier. *Plantains and capsicum work as coagulants. They help stop bleeding. And plantains are delicious, besides. Get well soon. Cal.*

Cal? Laid-back is not the word for him these days. I'd better start saving for a wedding present.

Slowly the days creep past. Slowly I heal. Bob writes almost daily. Texas is incredible; basic training is even more incredible; the number of push-ups he can do now is most incredible. But the most most most incredible thing of all is that he misses me incredibly. (I am so glad that he can't see me, black and blue and swollen-faced.) He's all right. He's surviving. There are even some possibilities for photography. He's saving for a camera.

Kate answers his letters for me the first couple of days after the operation, when I don't feel up to much. Then I take over. Eleven A.M. when the postman comes is the peak of the day. I can't wait for Sundays to be over; there's no mail on Sundays.

Once the swelling and bruising begin to go, Charlie

▼

is the first of the men to concede that my looks are improved, but he always has to add that all the money could have been better spent. Daddy says I'm beautiful, but I was beautiful before. And Grandpa? He says roughly that I no longer look like a Trevor at all. But I catch him sneaking looks at me and smiling, so I figure he can live with the nose. He doesn't hate it.

The time comes to go back to school. My face is mostly healed, but not completely. I certainly look different.

On the first day, I put on old jeans and a navy jersey and I do my hair and makeup as always. People can't help but notice my face change. I brace myself for what I know is coming.

Wouldn't you know, when I turn up the walk leading to school, which is fairly deserted — I stalled around until it was late, so I would miss the crowd — who do I practically trip over? Yes, there she is, Vickie Upham. Ditsy trendy Upham. Hot pink nails this time. Frazzled hairstyle and a micro-mini, skintight. Hurrying, because she's late, too, she glances over. "Annie?" I get the big stare. "Annie Trevor?"

Nodding coolly, I give her the brush and move along swiftly, but we are both heading for the same door and she is not letting me get away. No Bob to the rescue this time. He is in incredible Texas. I am on my own. I will have to handle her.

I slow down. She stumbles slightly at the sudden change of pace. "Whatever happened to your nose?" she asks.

Some people never learn.

"Whatever do you mean?" I give her innocent heavy blinking.

"You know what I mean."

"And you know what happened to my nose, Vicious Vickie. I had rhinoplasty. For those morons who don't know Greek that means a nose job. Plastic surgery."

"I only asked because you look so —"

"Pretty?" I supply the word. "Thanks for the admiration. My grandfather gave me this nose."

This scares her. She remembers that we had this same conversation before about my original nose. She thinks I've snapped my rubber band.

"That's what you said last time."

"Yeah. Grandpa gave me *that* nose, and he gave me this one, too."

"I'm late," she mumbles and takes off — fast.

Good riddance, I think. I move toward the gym and my locker so I can put my stuff away. I'm going to sit on the sidelines for a week, watching the others do heavy exercise. I have a medical note. It's one of the perks of the operation. I always wanted a medical note so I could be excused from gym.

Just finishing the lacing of her running shoes, Dee looks up at me, and she sees me and she isn't wearing glasses. "Annie!" she screams, and she hugs me. "You're beautiful. I swear. You're a movie star."

"So are you," I hug her back, "but we're late. Let's go in together."

We open the heavy door. I feel pretty. I can live

▼

160

with other people's stares and questions.

I think about Bob. I am looking forward to writing to him tonight and telling him about Vickie, and about how I am positive that she will never bring up the subject of my pet rhino again.

ABOUT THE AUTHOR

When writing *Rhino*, Sheila Solomon Klass was inspired by how tough it is for a teenager to take pride in his or her appearance. Ms. Klass writes, "*Rhino* grew out of my awareness of the difficulty many teenagers have in being comfortable with the way they look. They so much need to feel confident and pretty. (I was a teenage girl myself!)"

Ms. Klass is the mother of a family of widely read authors. Her older daughter, Dr. Perri Klass, is a well-known novelist and essayist. David Klass, her son, is author of the young adult novel *Wrestling with Honor*, which was published by Scholastic Point. Judy Klass, her younger daughter, is the author of a well-received science fiction novel and a collection of poetry.

Ms. Klass is a professor of English at Manhattan Community College. She has written eleven other books for adults and young adults, including *Credit-Card Carole*, *Page Four*, *The Bennington Stitch*, *Alive and Starting Over*, and, most recently, *Kool Ada*. This is her second book for Scholastic Hardcover.

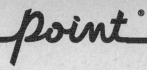

Other books you will enjoy,
about real kids like you!

☐ MZ42599-4	**The Adventures of Ulysses**	Bernard Evslin	**$4.50**
☐ MZ48467-2	**Calling on Dragons**	Patricia C. Wrede	**$4.50**
☐ MZ45722-5	**Dealing with Dragons**	Patricia C. Wrede	**$4.50**
☐ MZ43715-1	**Escape from Warsaw**	Ian Serraillier	**$3.50**
☐ MZ40943-3	**Fallen Angels**	Walter Dean Myers	**$4.50**
☐ MZ44479-4	**Flight #116 Is Down**	Caroline B. Cooney	**$3.99**
☐ MZ44110-8	**The Greek Gods**	Evslin and Hoopes	**$3.50**
☐ MZ43136-6	**Missing Since Monday**	Ann M. Martin	**$2.95**
☐ MZ42792-X	**My Brother Sam Is Dead**	James Lincoln Collier	**$3.99**
☐ MZ45721-7	**Searching for Dragons**	Patricia C. Wrede	**$3.25**
☐ MZ44651-7	**Sarah Bishop**	Scott O'Dell	**$3.50**
☐ MZ47157-0	**A Solitary Blue**	Cynthia Voigt	**$3.99**
☐ MZ42412-2	**Somewhere in the Darkness**	Walter Dean Myers	**$3.50**
☐ MZ43486-1	**Sweetgrass**	Jan Hudson	**$3.50**
☐ MZ48475-3	**Talking to Dragons**	Patricia C. Wrede	**$3.99**
☐ MZ42460-2	**To Be a Slave**	Julius Lester	**$3.50**
☐ MZ43638-4	**Up Country**	Alden R. Carter	**$2.95**
☐ MZ43412-8	**Wolf by the Ears**	Ann Rinaldi	**$3.50**

Watch for new titles coming soon!
Available wherever you buy books, or use this order form.

Scholastic Inc., P.O. Box 7502, 2931 E. McCarty Street, Jefferson City, MO 65102-7502

Please send me the books I have checked above. I am enclosing $ _____ .
Please add $2.00 to cover shipping and handling. Send check or money order– no cash or C.O.D.s please.

Name _____ Birthday _____

Address _____

City _____ State/Zip _____

Please allow four to six weeks for delivery. Offer good in U.S.A. only. Sorry, mail orders are not available to residents of Canada. Prices subject to change.

PNT795